To Miss Nettie Jean Jackson for planting the seed and to Chris, for watering it.

ISBN: 978-09843477-9-7

Library of Congress number 2014953377

Fiction : Short Stories (single author), Fiction : Fantasy - Short Stories
Author: C. Frazier Jones
Layout and Design: Jera Foster-Fell

Things We Thought We Saw in the Water is a collection of short stories. In these eight mesmerizing tales, author C. Frazier Jones takes us to a playground built by imagination, where mermaids ferry the dead to the the afterlife, a husband, long missing, returns as a cat and a vengeful spirit haunts a Pawnee, Oklahoma Walmart, much to the inconvenience of both customers and staff.

Published by Web Profile/Foster-Fell publications, Wolcott VT

Printed in the USA by Lightning Source.

Things We Thought We Saw in the Water

Deep Well

Jasper was in the well; this was something Marcus knew. So were Cookie and Buford, Elsie too, but of Gertrud, he could not be sure. Gertrud was a wanderer, among chicken kind a great explorer, who at times would be gone for weeks on end, often assumed dead, only to return by the light of the full moon or in the middle of a downpour and in need of assistance with a cut, scrape or any number of random and mysterious injuries that often lead Marcus to ask the chicken, *what in the world happened to you this time, Gertrud.* So Marcus was not all that concerned about Gertrud, she might be in the well or she might not. It was simply to early to tell about her, but of the others he was sure.

"How can you be so sure?" the sheriff asked.

"Well," started, Marcus. He had seen the chicken murders happen, but was ashamed to admit his almost completely passive role in the whole affair. So he started off with an observation, a safe way to leave himself out of the blame. "They're in there, you can stand over the edge and see them. They're piled up because there isn't enough water in there for them to float. I can't tell if Gertrud's underneath the others or not. It's too early to tell if she's gone adventuring or if she isn't."

The sheriff was a big man, well over six feet tall with the girth to match and when he shifted his weight from foot to foot, a habit he'd invented to give himself the feeling of escape when perceiving himself to be stuck, Marcus thought of "Jack and the Beanstalk." The end of the story where Jack chops down the beanstalk with his ax and the giant, no doubt struggling with shifting feet himself, becomes well acquainted with death. Marcus was sure the introduction of the giant's body to the earth must have left a deep crater, a fissured place bound into service for collecting rain. Mother Nature, in her infinite wisdom, would be well inclined to fill a cavity so ripe with potential.

Mother would direct the birds of the air to bring fish eggs and the spurs of plants upon their wading feet. To the frogs, she would whisper of the fertility of the place knowing full well that these eager, bouncing creatures, one of nature's most pragmatic of species, would oblige, wasting no time in tadpoling.

Pretty soon the whole body of water would team with abundance; fawns would drink, ducklings would swim, turtles would snap, beavers would dam. The memory of the dead giant would forever be banished beneath Mother's immoderate gift of life and the whole natural world would be better for it. Marcus liked to think so anyway.

The shuffling of the sheriffs feet was the sole indication that he would depart both shortly and abruptly. Marcus had dealt with Sheriff Tate enough times now to know this and so resigned to settle the matter quickly, even if it meant telling on himself.

"I saw them do it, Sheriff. They chased the chickens around the yard and when they caught them, threw them down the well. I think they'd been doing this for some time before I saw them. That's why I'm not sure if Gertrud is down there or not. "

The sheriff shifted again, then leaned back against the fence. So rotten were most of the posts holding the pickets that Marcus wondered if in its dilapidated state, the fence would hold the big man. The barrier creaked beneath his weight, and the Sheriff, now looking down at the boards beside him, narrowed his eyes in a way as to suggest a dare.

"What are you doing here, Marcus?" he asked, taking his eyes from the fence and returning them to Marcus.

"What do you mean, Sheriff Tate?"

"What I mean, Marcus, is I've known you since the day you were born. And I watched you grow up. You were a good kid and your mother and father worked harder than anything I've ever seen to send you to that school in Boston. They were so proud that you didn't have to live here where you didn't want to. But now they're gone, and here you are, taking up residence in a place you know you don't belong and causing trouble. So I'll ask you again, what are you doing here, Marcus?"

It was a confusing series of statements and questions. Especially since Marcus, himself had not thrown his own chickens down the well to die, but the neighbor children had; so why was he in trouble now and not them? In response to the sheriffs confounding narrative, Marcus came up with a series of his own.

"Why am I in trouble, Sheriff? I didn't do in my own chickens, those Collier kids did. Why do people like that get to go around hurting innocent people, or in this case, innocent chickens?"

The sheriff sighed, stood up straight from the fence.

"You know that those Collier kids throwing your chickens down that well of yours, which by the way should have been filled in years ago, is about the least offensive, illegal thing those boys have done this week. Call me back when they burn down your house, then we'll talk."

The two men stood there for a time staring into the others eyes. Finally, the sheriff offered his hand. Marcus took it.

"What do you want with chickens anyway?" the big man asked.

Marcus said he guessed what anybody did; companionship, eggs. The sheriff asked if they ever laid for him, to which Marcus said no, so far they hadn't. The moment with the sheriff seemed rushed and Marcus felt cheated that there was no time for reflection, not a single second to add to the conversation, *and now they never will because they're dead.*

"Get that well filled in before something else happens, Marcus," the sheriff instructed, opening the door to his car and lowering himself down onto the faux leather seat where he began the series of movements necessary to fulfilling his escape fantasy; shutting the door, strapping the belt across his chest, putting the car in *drive.* "Before something real bad happens."

Those were the sheriff's parting words. Marcus brought his hand up to wave, but it was too late. The sheriff was gone.

That night was the first time he saw her. She stood beside the well pulling chains of daisies from its depth. Thinking her one of the neighbor children, Marcus asked the girl who she was, a question she never bothered to answer. Instead, she concentrated on the well and the daisies, her ambitions like that of a magician pulling an endless supply of conjoined silks from a hat.

When a cloud would pass over the moon the girl would shimmer, her body fading in and out, caught between the phases of there and not so there. Perplexed, Marcus watched her. Was she real? A dream? An invention of the drink he held in his hand? Marcus didn't think so. From the porch he called to her.

"What are you doing?" he asked.

"Pulling them out," she answered, her downward stare fixated on the inner circle of well.

If he was perplexed before, and he was, he was even more so now. Pulling out the daisies? Pulling out the chickens? With the chains of daisies? If so, how would the chickens hold on? With their beaks? Impossible. And anyway, the chickens were certainly dead now.

"They're chickens," he told her, hoping that the information would somehow persuade and that the daisies would run out of length and that he would close his eyes and then open them and the specter girl would have given up the bizarre saving quest and gone away. Just gone away.

"There's something else," she answered back, never taking her eyes from the well. "There's something else."

He spent the night watching her from what he deemed a suitable distance from there on the porch until sleep forcibly came. When the sun came up and Marcus opened his eyes, the sparkling girl was gone.

Later that morning, he phoned the sheriff. "What do you know about that old well in my yard?" he asked, not bothering to identify himself. The sheriff cleared his throat. Marcus could hear a burdened chair squealing under the weight of the prodigious man. He imagined the chair to be antique, circa nineteen-thirties, solid wood and ladder backed; the kind you might see in a movie in which newspaper men wearing stiff, white shirts corralled by wide, patterned ties would travel typewriter to typewriter pounding out scoops and shouting phrases like, *"get it to the presses, fast!,"* and *"we've got em' now, boys!"*

Marcus had no idea if his impression of the chair was true at all, but he hoped so. The sound of the sheriff's voice suddenly coming through the phone helped put the wonderment aside.

"Well, I know its got four, possibly five dead chickens down it."

Marcus didn't bite at the joke. "What's that story?" he asked.

"What story?" The Sheriff cleared his throat again. Marcus wondered if he was coming down with a cold and looked at his own hand trying to remember if he had washed immediately after shaking the sheriff's hand the day before. "Summer colds are the worst," his mother used to say, "no matter where you spend your summer."

"The girl that drowned in the well, that story. My mother told me about it, but I can't remember much, honestly, I wasn't really listening." He was becoming better at confessions.

"Well, Marcus, a lot of people said that it happened that way, some people said it didn't, so what do I know?" It wasn't really a question, but Marcus treated it as one anyway.

"You know a lot more than I do. You were at least alive when it happened."

The sheriff cut him off.

"Marcus, I would have been six years old-was six years old."

"That's still better than what I know. I wasn't even born." The silence on the other end of the line was so profound that Marcus wondered if the sheriff had simply hung up, but when he heard the chair complain yet again, knew that the line still held.

"Sheriff?" he asked, but not really, "I want to know." The sheriff let out a deep breath; the chair absolutely screamed.

"I'll come see you after work, Marcus." the sheriff said, then hung up the phone.

The two men sat on the steps of the porch drinking a couple of import beers. Though the porch was wide and accommodating, Marcus hadn't bought any new furniture, so far being satisfied with the simple, uncluttered look he'd achieved after hauling away the rotting chairs and rusted metal glider; all leftover staples of his parents. The sheriff listened intently to Marcus's story, the whole time staring down at the slice of lime in his bottle, an addition that Marcus had insisted upon even though the sheriff had not. When Marcus was finished, the sheriff started in on a story of his own.

"What I know about it is this: The girl you describe? Sounds like the one who lived here. Had a good-for-nothing step-daddy who was mean as a snake. One night, he attacked the mama and beat her unconscious. There were two children, the girl, like I said, and the baby. Baby was a boy, if I recall correctly. Don't know his name, but the girl was Dorey; I remember that well. We were in the same class at school. She was a sweet, pretty little thing. Real petite, real shy. Had a smile that could crack a hard boiled egg.

Anyway, the stepdaddy threw Dorey down the well. Don't know if it was the fall that killed her or the water. Nobody does. He threw the baby out in the woods and something got it, most likely a pack of dogs, maybe even a coyote. While the mama was still out, he cut her throat from ear to ear."

"Good God," Marcus said, under his breath. The sheriff, ignoring the theology, moved on.

"With a shot gun and a pistol ready, the stepdaddy holed up in this very house. All that carnage everywhere, just laying there all over the ground and down in the well." The sheriff paused here and shook his head, a way of indicating that for him, the worst was yet to come.

Anyway, he was waiting, knowing that soon somebody would miss Dorey from school or the mama from work. He was right, eventually someone did. It was our first grade teacher, Ms. Duffy, that after two days of absence reported Dorey missing. I remember, I was real worried about her. I liked Dorey a lot, but I already told you that.

The sheriff at the time, Sheriff Clausen, came out here

to have a look and found the mama on the ground having succumbed to all the filth that goes with dying hard and being left out to rot. He yelled for the children but no one answered. He called on the radio for backup, then came up to the house here and knocked on the door. No sooner than he had, did the stepdaddy shoot him clean through it-damn near blew off his entire face. Poor son of a bitch was dead before he hit the ground." The sheriff paused here, turned up his beer. Marcus did the same, attempting to swallow the last bit of liquid left in his own bottle, but found it to be almost impossible for the lump in his throat.

"I don't know what makes a man behave the way that one did. I've wondered about it for years. Did somebody hurt him somehow, make him that way or was it just the way he chose to be? Or maybe he born that way. I guess we'll never know." The sheriff tapped his bottle on the tip of his boot, cleared the lump from his own throat, drummed his fingers against the wooden column beside him. The sheriff, it turned out, was a musical man.

"I don't doubt that you saw something, Marcus. I don't know what it was exactly, but I wouldn't go messing with it. My best advice to you is to have that well filled in. Should have been done years ago. I cannot imagine why it wasn't. If I had been sheriff then, I would have insisted on it." The sheriff stood and dumped out the remainder of his beer. Marcus judged the amount to be about half a bottles worth.

The sheriff extended his hand. Marcus stood and took it.

In silence, the two men walked to the patrol car. The sheriff slid in behind the wheel, shutting the door behind him. The engine turned on the first try, purring in newness and proficiency, a contradiction to its surroundings; the rotten fence, the dead chickens, the naked, sanitized porch. Marcus squatted down beside the car and spoke to the sheriff through the open window.

"I've been thinking about what you asked me yesterday, sheriff."

"Oh?" Sheriff Tate asked, flipping the switch for the head lights and illuminating the ground in front of the car, the crushed granite making up the driveway sparkling as if under a spell.

"Yea, about why I came back here. It's because of a tomato." The sheriff smiled, possibly for the first time in his life. "That must have been one hell of a tomato, to make a man leave New York City for this place." The sheriff waved his hand around, highlighting the state of ruin surrounding them.

"It was Brooklyn," Marcus corrected, knowing that last part didn't matter to anyone but a true New Yorker. To an outsider all of Manhattan and its burrows were New York. But to a New Yorker, only Manhattan was New York.

"Brooklyn," the sheriff repeated, nodding his head. "Go on."

"I read a newspaper article about a truck hauling tomatoes in Florida. Somewhere around in Dade County I think, Miami area, green tomatoes on their way to a chemical house to be ripened. The truck had some sort of trouble and turned over on the highway, all of the tomatoes spilling with it. And here's the thing Sheriff, not a one of those green tomatoes burst. Not one."

The sheriff interrupted.

"Sure, they're hybrids. Tomatoes made for shipping-not particularity good for eating. Everybody knows that. Why do you think we look so forward to summer round here. It ain't the heat, son, it's the tomatoes."

"I know all that, but Sheriff, not a one of those tomatoes broke, not one split, not even a dent." The sheriff shifted his weight in the seat and put his hand on the gear shift; signs indicative of an imminent departure. Marcus, remembering the last unrequited wave between himself and the sheriff, decided to bring the point home.

"I read that article and thought to myself that I could do better than that, so I bought a tomato plant, put it on my fire escape and guess what?" It was the part of the speech inviting participation, but the sheriff remained silent. Undeterred, Marcus went on. "I couldn't do better. I planted that tomato plant exactly according to the directions given on the tag. I watered it, I fertilized it, I fussed over it. I even got blooms, tons of blooms. But when they fell off, no fruit. Not one measly tomato, just bright yellow blossoms of nothingness."

"You need bees to set the fruit. Do they have bees in *Brooklyn*?" There was a lilt to the man's voice that came across as predatory, smug. If there had been a smile, the comment could have been construed as good natured, regional ribbing. But there was no smile, and Marcus perceiving an oncoming war, had no time to temper his response. From him a reply rushed organically; a condition without thought.

"I pollinated them myself, with one of Johnathon's paintbrushes." In Brooklyn, in Marcus's circle of friends, it would have been was the right response; the thing to say to garnish sympathy and sway the outcome of any battle in Marcus's favor. But this was rural Georgia and Sheriff Tate a man of another generation. A man on whose wrinkled forehead could be imagined the accumulation of years of conflict, dislike and distrust. Marcus couldn't be sure of his response.

Sheriff Tate shifted his feet around the narrow space of the floorboard, one foot finding the brake pedal and pumping it; behind them, the rear light glowing red and pulsating, high-lighting the soundless emergency.

"I'm sorry about your friend," he said, looking straight ahead. "That's not right, not a fair thing." The sheriff became quiet, the words that moments before had poured so easily, so freely, now dried up like Marcus's dreams of tomatoes on the fire escape in Brooklyn.

Marcus stood and kicked at a rock. The sheriff shifted the car into drive. Somewhere a line had been crossed, but in reverse, tenderness poured out so freely, so naturally, both men were alarmed and disconcerted, their shared silence serving as the proof. It was the sheriff who finally breached the uncomfortable place between them.

"So, it sounds like you're planning on starting some toma-toes then? It's not too late, you know. Macon county has all the bees you could need-no paint brush required here." The words were meant as a truce, the sheriff smiling as he offered them.

Marcus accepted. He reached through the car window and took the sheriff's hand again. It felt good to touch another human-he hadn't in so long. The feeling made Marcus feel somehow even more human, and as he shook the sheriff's hand he found himself being persuaded. Persuaded from what he thought he knew about old men in Georgia, of men who serve as deacons in Baptist churches, men in uniform who judge other men, arrest them, carry a gun and know how to use it. In spite of years of self conditioning otherwise, he found that he liked the sheriff.

"I don't know, we'll see," Marcus grinned, giving the sheriff's hand a final shake.

The gravel crunched under the tires of the patrol car. "Fill up that well, Marcus," sang the sheriff, his voice dancing back down the driveway; the only melody the music man left behind.

Well into the night Marcus sat on the porch and waited for the dead girl, but she never showed. Sometime after three he fell into bed and under the trance of dreaming finally saw the ghost and her daisies; the cheerful flowers of a one-sided tug-of-war weaved into chain after chain after chain. Marcus woke up laughing. Never in his life had he dreamed of a girl, yet now he did. The conditions of the dream were fitting, he supposed. This female fantasy was safe for even a gay man to embrace, for she was dead as a doornail and forever six years old.

When the phone rang, Marcus answered with a "Hello, Sheriff."

"You must have that, Caller ID," came the reply.

"No, just a hunch. What can I do for you?" He heard the complainy chair in the background and wondered if he would someday be on the line when the tortured thing finally collapsed and what that would sound like.

"Listen, I was thinking. About your well. A friend of mine over at the highway department has a truck load full of pulled up asphalt and dirt leftover from a project. It's slated to go to the landfill, but it could go into that well of yours instead. What do you think?"

Marcus bit into a banana and chewing it said, "I don't know. I think something funny might be going on with that well."

"You eating?"

"Yep. I didn't think you'd mind."

"Well I do. Quit it. Your mother raised you better than that." Marcus laughed, but not because it wasn't true but because he couldn't imagine a man like the sheriff minding over such things as manners.

"Sorry, you're right," he said, laying the banana aside. "But, back to the well. I think something interesting is happening around that well."

"You talking about that ghost?"

"Yep." It was the second time he'd said "yep" in a very long time. Johnathon thought the word ridiculous and early on in their relationship had put a stop to it. Marcus didn't know from where this word was coming, his memory or his desire.

"All the more reason to fill it up, Marcus. Listen, people may laugh at me, but I think there are things that we can't understand, aren't even meant to understand and I don't play around with them. And, let us not ignore the facts. To complicate matters, you've got four, maybe five dead chickens down a well. A well, that thanks to one of the finest droughts in Georgia state history, has very little water in it and all that, in the, on average, ninety-five degree Georgia sun. Pretty soon, the stench of those birds is gonna run you right off your property and back to New York City. Excuse me, I mean *Brooklyn*."

Marcus smiled at what he now recognized as friendly

banter. "Alright, when can I expect the dirt?"

"Good man. I would think sometime this afternoon. I'll come out and help, bring a couple of sledge hammers, then we can knock the lip of the well down there too. After it's filled up you can put a table right on it, hold a séance or something, get your ghost that-a-way."

Marcus hung up the phone thinking about the girl and the dirt and the conjunction of the two and wondering if she would mind or not, being buried for the second time.

The sheriff arrived out of uniform wearing jeans and a T-shirt, the words on the back extolling the virtues of a mini-golf place located in Gulf Shores, Alabama. Reaching into the back of his truck, he took out two sledgehammers, handing one over to Marcus, while keeping the other for himself.

"You ready?" he asked. Marcus said that he was.

The dump truck driver had already come and gone, leaving Marcus with an enormous pile of dirt and chunks of broken asphalt. In order to get in close proximity to the well, the driver hadn't noticed the ragged fence surrounding the yard and had backed over it, leveling the entire thing beneath the massive tires of the truck. The man never acknowledged the mistake and Marcus, deciding a great favor had just been performed on his behalf, didn't bother pointing it out. He figured he'd throw what remained of his mother's beloved picket fence down into the well. "The more the merrier," he reasoned, adding the splintered pieces to the pile.

"I was thinking about your ghost, Marcus. How do you know it's Dorey?" the sheriff asked, tapping his hammer to the side of the well as if to test his strength against the resistance of the mortared rock.

"It has to be. How many other little girls were murdered in that well?"

"None other than the one that I know of, that's true. But, your ghost, she could be of the traveling variety; just passing through. She may have nothing to do with Dorey." This time he brought the sledge hammer down hard, the lip of the well crumbling beneath its force and spilling over into the hole. "Good," he said. "This won't be too bad, I don't think."

Marcus took a turn, his swing netting the same results. "Sheriff Tate, I was thinking. You do not strike me as the kind of man who would believe in ghosts, or at the very least admit to believing in ghosts."

The sheriff swung again. This time when he answered, his voice sounded strained, the words coming in stages and huffs. "I am too old, Marcus, to worry about, what, others, might think, about what, I think. And you, should call me, Henry."

It was Marcus's turn to swing. "Henry," he repeated the name, his voice sounding unsure, as if he were trying the name for a little while to see if it suited the man who owned it. He brought down the hammer, the blow landing slightly to the right of his intended target, the uneven edge of the well catching the head of the tool in a way that nearly sent Marcus to the ground. He recovered and took another swing, this one landing soundly on target, the stone and mortar crumbling into a powdery rain.

"Henry it is then, but I have to tell you, I've always had such a hard time calling my father's friends by their first names. Somehow it just doesn't seem right." He took another swing, this one intentionally out of turn in order to give Henry a chance to catch his breath.

"That's the Georgia boy in you, Marcus. Good manners. It's true what they say. It's hard to out run your raising." The sheriff reclaimed his turn, this time bringing his hammer up and in an arc over his head. When landed, the force of the blow shattered what remained of the top scape of the well, creating a fissure, the final pieces of rock caving beneath the scar.

The men dropped their hammers to the ground and kicked at the remains, feet punching slowly, steadily, moving rock and broken mortar past the cliff of the well and down into the hole.

To Henry, this landscape revision helped in re-affirming, if not increasing, his manhood. But even more than that, reminding him that he was a person still alive and with a few more blows left to deliver. He remembered the change of his own father, a steady decline of both spirit and health beginning around the age of seventy; Henry's current age. Being this old worried him. Sometimes the anxiety of his own, unavoidable decline woke him in the night, temporarily paralyzing his sleeping until a random, unrelated thought would pop into his head, bringing him back to a more reasonable, productive state of thinking. A place in which he would remember to turn on the lamp beside him, the illumination providing a way to look upon the face of the wife he still adored. It was in those moments that Henry Tate sorted, distinguishing the good-her lying there beside him, the gentle, rhythmic sounds of her breathing, from the bad--his age, hers, the stroke that contorted the even shape of her still lovely face leaving one plain slightly but noticeably higher than the other.

It was in the glow of the lamp that he remembered his religion, praying that she would be taken before him, that his health would last to see the both of them through. And it was in the darkness that he lost it, a deep well of blackness swallowing his hopes, the things that he wanted to, but couldn't quite believe.

"I think we're ready for the dirt and such," Henry said. "And whatever else you want to put down this hole."

Marcus considered the statement, and after a moment of contemplation, found it to be loaded. But for the blank look on the sheriff's face, he judged it to be troublesome only to himself. If only filling up a hole with whatever you wanted, or didn't want, was that simple, that easy. If murdered lovers were rotten fence post and parents who pretended they were okay with your "choices" but really, were not, were shattered rock, then one *could* push them down to the bottom of a hole, filling the empty space inside. Put enough down that hole and eventually, surely, a level place would form on top above the ground where on could stand, maybe even stomp.

But dead lovers were not fences and parents were not rocks and holes were as permanent today, and as far as Marcus could tell, would be tomorrow, because try as he may, he had no idea how to fill the deep well inside him. The hole that gaped and called, the one that kept him up at night with a drink in his hand and a tear in his eye. Henry was wrong. One could out run one's raising, but out running one's living was another thing entirely.

For the next hour the men threw hand and shovel loads of unwanted things down the well, layering each cast off as if

it were an ingredient in a carefully planned trifle. Fence post
and picket, dirt, asphalt. Repeat. Repeat. Repeat.

The next morning Marcus stood on the porch surveying
the yard, the well now gone. The absence of the structure and
the newness of the red clay topping the ground in its place
proved to be such a distraction that several minutes went by
before he noticed the sprawl of spray paint across the side of
his car; *Faggot*. His stomach dropped. He walked over and
placed his hand upon the word, the letters burning beneath
his fingers. He wished he could cause their disintegration
with just his touch.

When darkness fell he thought of Henry's joke of putting
a table atop the mound; a facility for conjuring up the dead.
The exercise proved to be unnecessary as the specter girl
came without prompting. She sat Indian style upon the death
mound, her fingers carefully unlacing the seemingly endless
daisy chain. A flock of chickens surrounded her, some Marcus
recognized as the recently departed, some he didn't. One by
one she took the daisies apart, slowly dissecting them with
her hands.

"He loves me, he loves me not," she explained to the chickens, delicately placing a petal into each receptive beak. One
bird after another came, carefully taking her love, leaving the
girl empty handed.

Marcus had never seen chickens be so attentive, so solic-
itous. Something swelled inside him, something familiar,
something he thought, akin to love. But was the affection for
the chickens, so thoughtful in their taking, or for the girl, so

generous in her giving? He shook the question off, waving to her instead.

"We filled in the well. I hope you don't mind." The girl ignored him but for some reason he couldn't quite discern, he continued to wave. Soon he began to feel like an idiot, like the poor retarded kid everyone feels sorry for who refuses to quit waving even after the final length of parade has passed and Santa and his reindeer are nothing but a tiny speck down the street. He lowered his hand but unsure of his resolve, stuffed both in his pockets, then walked down the three short steps of the porch. He was six feet away from her now, maybe seven.

"I feel like you need my help. Can I help you? Is there something that you need?" He squatted where he stood. They were now eye level, if she would only look his way.

"I like Popsicles," she told Marcus, never taking her eyes from the daisies or the chickens. "You have any of those?"

"I'm sorry, I don't." He made a mental note to pick some up the next time he went into town. She didn't respond to the disappointment, but instead continued on with the tearing of the petals and the feeding of the hens. As he watched her, Marcus rocked back and forth on his heels, an attempt to prolong the unsustainable pose.

It popped into his head and he couldn't stop himself from asking.

"Do you know that you're dead?"

She dropped the chain and looked up. For the first time, Marcus saw her eyes. The rocking stopped. He sat paralyzed, unable to move.

"Yep. Dead as a doornail."

His legs would no longer hold him in the squatting position

and as he fell back into the yard, a panic like he had never know crept up his spine, a feeling so bridling he felt at once himself a doll controlled by an unseen handler; a phantom drawing his shoulders up to meet the base of his neck and by string binding them there.

He hung his head, ashamed, but wanted nothing else to do with the girl.

"I'm sorry. I'm so sorry. I have to go." He found his feet and on them rushed in the direction of the house. With one giant leap he covered the steps but when he got to the door, somehow, she had beat him to it and now stood there blocking his way. Marcus let out a scream that he could only imagined sounded like that of a little girl itself. He threw his hand in front of his mouth hoping to plug the ridiculous, gaping hole.

"Hey mister, why did those kids throw your chickens down the well in the first place? And why did they write that stuff on your car? And why did you give hens boy names? Do you even know anything about chickens at all?" Now it was the girl who rocked back and forth on her heels, the daisies, somehow restored back into the chain swaying endlessly in her hands, creating a hypnotically, dizzying effect. He reached past her to open the door.

"Thank you," she said politely, walking in before him. "And let me tell you, those boys next door are trouble and I know trouble. They're mean, like my stepdaddy. I hate mean." She sat down on the couch and wiggling back into the cushions, crossed her arms over her chest. Marcus recognized the posture; the girl was hunkering down for a chat. He shut the door behind him, then took a seat opposite her in the rocker, where immediately, he surrendered his head to his hands.

"I'm always cold," she said, running her hands over the velvet fringe of a pillow. "But, I can see things now that I couldn't see before."

"Like what?" he asked, careful not to look into her eyes. He could taste bile in his mouth, feel a knot of it forming in his throat. He fought the urge to expel.

She shrugged her shoulders up and down. The simple, innocent act making her seem like even more of a child, and with it a sudden wave of pity for the general population of the world's youthful dead washed over him. Not only the children of murder, but of famine, disease, war, land mines. Did that last one even happen anymore?

Early in his and Jonathon's relationship, the two of them had attended the premier of a documentary on the Vietcong and the things they left behind, specifically limbless children. Marcus had been a graduate student at the time and was still fresh enough off the literal farm that he still remembered feeling particularly glamorous, joyful and liberated that evening, for the first time openly attending an event with a boyfriend. But after watching the film, he felt ashamed, despondent, foolish. In light of such evil he knew his joy should be contained and that these gamut running feelings could never go together, that such opposite emotions were not meant to mingle.

"I shouldn't be happy tonight, out of respect for those children," he told Jonathon as they left the event together. Jonathon didn't attempt to touch him that night and though he did sleep over, kept to himself on the couch sharing the space with an openly hostile cat named Purgatory, but called Gator for convenience.

It was on the heel of that memory that Marcus decided Dorey too deserved his respect and that his own weaknesses, his own limitations rooted in fear, should not keep him from giving her fully what she deserved. He vowed to face her, eye to eye. With exorbitant effort, the line of his eye traveled from the place of her general direction and landed squarely upon her face.

Dorey smiled. "Peek a boo. I see you," she giggled.

He could not return the smile.

Suddenly, it hit him! Surely, he had lost his mind and was now, certifiably, indisputably crazy. Now his fear wasn't so much rooted in the undeniable torment brought by Dorey's eyes, but of the realization that the scene in which he found himself the principle player was completely absurd. He couldn't have written anything more unreal, more sinister had he tried and trying was his job, or had been before Jonathon was murdered, the tomato truck spilled somewhere in Florida, his chickens were killed, the well filled and the word faggot appeared, sprawled across the side of his car, written by someone so obviously unashamed to do such loathsome work, that the rolling, optimistic hills of the letters only served in confirming the pure joy exercised in the expression of leaving such hate.

He sat in the chair that once was his mothers favorite, rocking back and forth in this new revelation, listening to the squeak of the gliders punctuate the girls routine. "Peek a boo, I see you," repeated Dorey, in between the back and forth noise. *Peek a boo, I see you*, became the words to the melody of the chair. Marcus kept his eyes shut tight as the devilish song filled up the night.

Morning came and with it another revelation: four punctured tires, one still seeping, a sound remarkable in its release as Marcus was sure he heard the hissing rubber squeal, *help*, as the final bit of air left that prison.

Later when Henry knocked on the front door, Marcus, craving solitude in his newly discovered insanity, didn't answer, hoping that the sheriff would give up and go away. But he wouldn't and through the glass partition of the door explained why not.

"Look Marcus, you might as well open the door. I've seen your car and I know you couldn't possibly be anywhere but here, so open up." The announcement came, accompanied by an long series of fist banging.

"Marcus," the sheriff now sang, "get up off your carcass and open, open, the door."

The delight of the rhyme was apparent as the sheriff's voice trolled on over the lyrics two, then three more times. Marcus rolled out of bed, slid his feet into his slippers. He might be crazy he surmised, but he still didn't walk bare-footed on floors; never had, never would. Oddly, he'd always thought, his position on the matter to be one of the reasons to which his own father had pointed as proof enough that Marcus didn't belong in Georgia, but some far away and glamorous city like Paris, France or Hoboken, New Jersey.

"What the Hell happened to you?" Henry sputtered as Marcus opened the door. Marcus took a moment to rub the sleep from his eyes before answering.

"I had a bad night, and when I woke up, my morning didn't look that much better so I went back to bed." He turned his back to the sheriff and took off back down the hall to his bedroom where he removed an old terry cloth bath robe from a hook on the wall. He heard Henry banging around in the kitchen and took off in that direction. When he got there, he found the sheriff loading ground coffee into the machine and searching through the upper cabinets for mugs.

"The one to the left of the sink," Marcus instructed, sitting down at the table. Cold chills ran up and down the length of his body; his arms burned singularly, then plurally with apprehension, raw nerves. His stomach ached and he found himself thinking of his mother and the way she would drop whatever she was doing to dote on him when he was ill; pressing a cool cloth to his head, singing hymns, telling stories about princess's and brave knights, a North African jinn and a clever, buoyant fox.

"Marcus, what we have here is a hate crime, plain and simple." The sheriff found the mugs and set them down, then went back to humming about around the machine. "Now, you and me know its those good for nothing Collier boys, but unless you saw them do it, we don't have any proof, so here's what I propose. I'm gonna set up a game camera-I've got one in the trunk of the car. It's infrared, so it can see everything that happens, even in the dark and then, bam!, when those boys come over here tonight to do their mischief making, we've got them on tape. Yes sir, we've got those old boys now, Marcus."

The machine beeped, professing readiness. "Mmm mmm, that smells good," the sheriff purred. He filled the two cups and sat down opposite Marcus at the table, handing him the mug reading, "World's best Dad," in bold, blue letters across the front. Marcus brought the cup to his lips and winced at the heat. The sheriff did the same and as both men struggled to drink from the pot of something that should so obviously be allowed time to cool, Henry drummed lively, nimble fingers on the surface of the table, a tune familiar to Marcus but not so much that he could place it.

"You really look terrible, Marcus. I think you may be sick," Henry said, reaching across the table to touch Marcus's forehead with the back of his hand. Marcus immediately sank under the tender weight of the sheriff's hand, slumping forward and landing on his elbows. "You're burning up, man!" Henry spewed. "How long has this been going on?"

Marcus couldn't say. He suspected the fever came on about the time of Dorey's last cryptic visit, the point at which he discovered his own mental faculties defecting. But as with all betrayals, he really didn't know. He shrugged his shoulders up and down, like Dorey the dead girl had the night before; like a thousand other dead girls before her. The act came to him naturally, because, he supposed now more than ever, he felt like a helpless child.

The arcing up and down of Marcus shoulders made Henry ache in a way he had not in years. He had seen that movement before, had once held a child close as he made that move. *"Why did you break Mommy's lamp, James? Why did you run from me when I called you?"* And later, when the child was older, *"Why James, why do you do this to your mother? She's a good woman and she doesn't deserve these things. Don't you know its wrong to steal from your own mother? James, don't you know you're killing yourself, killing all of us?"*

These were the all too familiar questions of James Tate's short life, spanning the time from about his fourth birthday to the day before he disappeared from Henry and Lydie's life forever, just one day shy of his twenty-second birthday. Henry would never forget that day; May seventeenth, 1995. While other kids Jame's age were graduating from college, falling in love, planning extraordinary, useful lives, James Tate, the one and only beloved child of Lydie and Henry Tate, was busy dying alone from an overdose behind a dumpster in a back alley of Atlanta's club district.

Lydie preached her own consolation to Henry, telling him that James wasn't alone; God was there. "God never leaves us alone," she would explain when the mood for evangelizing would strike her, which was pretty much all the time for a good three years after James's death.

The sheriff consoled himself in another way; through reason. They had done everything right, he and Lydie, raised James gently but firmly, taught him right from wrong, had taken him to church, loved him, educated him, provided for him always. This was when the sheriff began to doubt the reason of God. Not God's reasons, but the reason people made up and worshiped a god, for now he knew that in that alley, but for the needle marks littering the darkened surfaces of his son's arms, James was alone; truly, hopelessly alone.

God had not been there, or Jesus or even an angel. And God had not been there because he had never been anywhere but in the imaginations of peoples miserable lives, the hopeless and hopeful alike, the weak and the strong.

Over the years the sheriff had softened, a different kind

of reason had come back to him, and hope. If there was no God, the spirit everyone claimed as being so genius, then who set this whole blooming mess of a planet into motion, anyway? Who laid the lazy rivers down across the red clay soil of Georgia, or the ocean at her edge, a place he and Lydie often drove hoping for sightings of dolphins and sea turtles. Who made the clouds and the sun, the moon and the stars? If he couldn't look to the heavens for these answers, then where could he look?

He could then concede some merit to this theory, but if God really existed, he could not forgive Him for leaving James alone. This was the condition for his belief; God could be real, but He could not be forgiven.

In Henry's mind, if God had wanted, The Great Lord himself could have reached down from Heaven and using the same finger he pointed Adam into existence, punched the numbers, *911*, into the worn down silver buttons of the pay phone positioned not ten feet away from where James took his final breath.

Every year on James's birthday, Henry re-visited the booth. He stood inside its narrow walls holding the receiver in his hand, the buzzing of the unhooked devise filling up the space, angry as ever that God hadn't punched in the numbers that could have saved his son, angry that no one had. It wasn't until his last visit to the booth that Henry realized that James himself had used that phone to order his final fix. That was when the sheriff had decided to let God off the hook; the choice had been James's all along.

"Let's get you back in bed, son," the sheriff said, standing and helping Marcus from his chair, his mind already searching the glove box of his patrol car for the aspirin and bottle of Pepto he kept inside. To the sheriff, every ailment could be virtually cured with one or both of these two treatments and he vowed to fix Marcus up, the way he had fixed himself up countless times before. He explained his plan to Marcus as he helped him down the hall, Marcus nodding his head the best he could, hoping to convey to the sheriff that he was willing to experiment in the hopes of achieving such a revival.

By the time the sheriff had Marcus medicated and tucked into bed with the covers pulled up to his chin, the workings of his mind had switched from nursing to the game camera, contemplating the best location to place it in order to capture the greatest potential expanse of the yard.

Marcus lay in bed, listening through the windows to the shuffling sounds of the sheriff out in the yard. Just from the symphonic partnership between his voice and his feet, Marcus could glean the whereabouts of each location that Henry was trying the camera. He wondered if the sheriff shouldn't be quiet as he worked. Could the Collier boys be spying on the big man now? Planning their way back into the yard for their next round of merriment? Plotting a route just outside the view of the lens?

This seemed to Marcus a sensible thought and not the reasonings of the mad man just a few hours before he'd assumed himself to be. And this worried Marcus. If he was rational and not crazy, did that mean that the girl was real? In order for the girl to be a mirage, he was more than willing to trade rational for crazy, but didn't know how or to whom such an arrangement could be made. Disheartened, he drifted off to sleep to the sound of the sheriff's progress reports reverberating throughout the yard.

No, that's no good. Maybe there, maybe there. In the Live Oak, in the Crepe Myrtle? No, that's no good, that's no good. Maybe there, maybe there?

So many possibilities, harmoniously tried.

When Marcus woke again he was drenched in sweat; his fever finally broken. His mother's rocking chair had been transported from down the hall and the sheriff now sat beside him, keeping watch over his sick bed. Darkness seeped in through the windows. Marcus asked the time.

"Young man, it's about eleven. I have just spoken to Lydie on the phone and she is playing bridge with Mrs. Trumble and will stay the night with her. So, I can sit here with you and we will wait and see, wait and see, what happens with those cameras." Henry rubbed his hands together as if warming them over an invisible fire sitting upon his lap, and humming a John Philip's Sousa tune that Marcus recognized from a underwhelming, one year stint in his middle school band. He had no idea who Mrs. Trumble was or why it was important that she stay with the sheriff's wife, but had no desire to ask. Being left so weak from the fever gave Marcus the feeling that listening and occasionally nodding his head were almost more than he should be expected to do.

"I have the camera set up, and I think pretty much out of sight. If those boys are gonna make a move, they won't be doing it unnoticed," Henry said, giving his own knee a preemptive victory slap.

It was then that the girl walked unceremoniously through the wall, her ever present chain of daisies now serving as a leash for the row of chickens she led in formation behind her.

The sheriff sprang from the chair but made no move to escape the room. Instead, he stood in front of the rocker, the gliders creaking back and forth, confirming his sudden departure; the macabre music of the night.

"My God," the sheriff quickly concluded.

Dorey, cocking her head to one side looked up at the sheriff and smiled.

"We used to go to school together. You were my sweetheart, Henry Tate."

"Dorey?" Henry asked, his voice somehow remarkably wet and dry at the same time. The girl smiled again as confirmation, this time deeper, a smile more real. If she hadn't have been so dead, the depth of her smile would have made her look very much alive.

"Dorey, I-I don't know what to say," the sheriff stammered, looking over at Marcus for help. "What's happening with her eyes? I don't understand it." Marcus did though, because when the fever had come, under its spell he had figured it out.

"She sees the future. What you see in her eyes-it's going to happen."

Silence hung round them like a shroud as the two men stared into her eyes. Pulling her chickens with her, Dorey stepped forward, closer to the men, the sockets of her eyes swelling and expanding; the orbs flashing in an eerie, revelatory glow. Henry backed up against the chair, sending it into a state of hysterical rocking. "Then we've got to get out of here," he said, reaching down and taking hold of Marcus's arm. "Forget about those damn shoes, Marcus," Henry scolded, as Marcus's groped underneath the bed with his toes.

The noise that followed sounded like an airplane hitting.

Marcus knew this because he had seen the second one hit the tower. He had run towards it thinking of nothing but Jonathon being inside, *his* Jonathon, who was working on a mural for an investment firm on the eighty-third floor. The assignment of the painting had been Jonathon's dream, one in which Marcus had joyfully shared. Outside the burning building, the police held him at arms length, where he was left with nothing else to do but watch the dream go up in smoke.

"Molotov Cocktail," Marcus announced unenthusiastically, as if answering an absurdly easy question on a less than spectacular game show. Flames chased away the darkness, filling the room with licking tongues of light. Marcus tried again for his shoes, the sheriff saying nothing this time but tired of this tedious pursuit, forcibly pulled him away from the bed and out the door of his childhood bedroom.

It was at this point that Dorey began to sing, the sweetness of her voice rising up like the new bird in spring. But it wasn't words that she sang, instead a series of clucks and mews; a way of talking to her birds. The chickens on their string began to circle the girl and as Dorey continued her avian calls, she became wrapped in the daisies, stamens popping like fireworks; a sensual yellow flush of pollen rushing from each center. In this time of fire, Dorey had begun a Maypole. It was then that Marcus knew; the dead were completely indifferent to the sufferings of the living.

The sheriff succeeded in pulling Marcus out into the hallway, but it was here that the house became a maze, the short distance between the various rooms swollen with smoke. Marcus felt around him, the blind in search of what was, but everything he touched was shrouded in the newness of heat and darkness, disguised beyond the imagination of his touch.

Windows exploded from one end of the house to the other, the Collier boys having found them all. There was no order to the explosions, and Marcus thought it remarkable how random and strange the distorted pattern of their breaking seemed; one to the back of him, another to the side, next, one at the front of the house, then one indistinguishable, somewhere in the middle. The riddle to this destruction surrounded him, a tangled equation he had no hope of solving.

"Henry Tate, you were my sweetheart," Dorey's voice echoed down the hall. The sentiment was too much and Henry screamed at the girl to stop. In the darkness he groped for Marcus's hand and when he found it, held on. The touch awakened a memory in Marcus, of his own mother leading him deep into the earth and into a shelter beneath their feet, a safe place from the storms that routinely visited Georgia come springtime. Marcus felt around with his naked foot and upon finding the notch cut for a handle, pulled the sheriff down with him. Together they lifted the door, then descended; Henry following Marcus down the steps into the waiting darkness, Marcus never letting go of his hand.

Dalia Peterson was reading through the nursing section of the Macon County Community College fall catalog when the call came through on the radio.

"Henry Tate was my sweetheart," said a girl, her voice springy and singsong, sweet and soft, like morning dew.

Dalia threw the catalog down beside a wadded empty cellophane wrapper that ten minutes before had housed a six pack of cheese crackers straight out of the lobby vending machine, grabbed the receiver and brought it so close to her mouth that she could almost taste the age of the yellowed, crackled plastic. "Come again?" she asked. "Over."

From the other end came a deep, penetrating sigh, then a repeat of the announcement. "Henry Tate was my sweetheart, but now, he's in a house of fire." Here the voice stopped. Dalia couldn't tell if the child was collecting her thoughts or creating new ones. Patience had never been one of the many virtues Dalia held dear. Self discipline, integrity, forgiveness, love even, but never patience. With her tongue, she felt a bit of cracker caught between her molar and her gum. Expertly, she worked it loose, spitting it across the room into the vast, empty space of the office. She was the only officer at the station that night, but the graveyard shift was never lonely. Shelby, her husband and the other night officer, was out on patrol. At the moment, she didn't know exactly where Shelby was cruising, but knew that he too would be listening to the call. "Who is this?" she demanded, eyes narrowing at the prospect of the call being a joke.

"Soon, he'll be dead like me," said the girl, substituting her state of being for identity. Dalia, an expert in prophecy herself, knew the girl would say no more. Quickly, she switched over to the private channel she and Shelby used to get each other through the night.

"You hear that, honey?" she asked.

"Sure did," came the reply. "Henry said he was going out to Marcus Hart's place to set up a game camera. I'm almost there." Shelby always got straight to the point which was fine with Dalia because more than anything in the world, she hated waste. Waste of money, opportunity, potential, waste of time. You name it, she hated to waste it. Shelby's ability to cut through the tape that would bind such idleness together was a virtue she truly admired.

"I'll send fire and ambulance. And honey," she paused here, the way she always did when affection was about to be delivered, "be careful. Over"

"Over," said the voice, just before the channel returned to static. Dalia now reached for the phone, fingers, through memory, dialing a number pad that had long ago worn away. She counted the rings as she waited for the transfer. After three, she got Tina on the line.

"Tina, I need fire and ambulance out at the Hart place, county road 240. Henry's out there."

"Good Lord, girl! I'm on it. But don't hang up, Johnson's got a rash."

Knowing this would take a while, Dalia leaned back in the chair, making herself comfortable. Being enrolled in nursing classes at the college made Dalia a valuable asset to any friendship, especially this one. Johnson, a mealy, pale child allergic to everything, always had a rash.

Shelby Peterson was not a man who panicked. In high school, he'd been voted, "most laid back," by members of the student body. In the yearbook, a depository for such superfluous memories, a picture exists of Shelby straddling a fence, a sash draped across his shoulders, the words informing the banner freshly poured from a bottle of glitter glue, gleaming, proclaiming him "easy." This photo was a gift to the entire class, all of whom immediately christened the image as that of their own "Easy Rider,"; a moniker so thick with sexuality and innuendo that by the end of the school year, the name Shelby was dead to his peers and the much preferred nick-name became forever immortalized with a tattoo burned onto his bicep.

With that tattoo, the Easy Rider had kept his cool through three tours of duty in Afghanistan, delivering the baby of a terrified non-English speaking, Hispanic teenager at a conve-nience store, multiple domestic disputes at the Whispering Pines Trailer Home Park, three armed robberies in prog-ress, too many angry speeders to count, most of whom were just passing through "this one horse town," on their way to Atlanta and delivering the eulogy of his own father, a man whom Shelby so keenly despised.

So when the Easy Rider pulled up to see the Hart home engulfed by flames, a yard full of miscreants throwing bottles of fire and a dead girl leading a string of chickens around by a chain made up entirely of daisies, it was not beyond the scope of his personality that he sat motionless in his patrol car a good fifteen seconds before muttering the word, "shit," then reluctantly exiting the car.

Behind him he could hear the wailings of the firetruck, a sound so vicious it seemed to split the night into sections; the time before Shelby arrived at the inferno, when he drove the back roads of the county thinking of Dalia and the nursery that together they had just painted a gender neutral green and the time after his arrival, when he knew he might not live long enough to father the child for whom the room was divined.

The Collier boys turned and upon seeing the law scattered, a trail of profanity leading them home. But the dead girl stayed. Calling the chickens to her side one by one, Dorey studied the lawman as he passed by in front of her.

"Henry Tate used to be my sweetheart," she called to the deputy as if to remind him; an attempt to keep up a conversation in which the two strangers had never engaged.

Shelby, ignoring the girl walked on, keeping his eyes fixed squarely on the burning building before him. Dorey blinked at his progress, the image of a laughing baby playing across the orbs of her eyes like a scene cast and divided between two separate movie screens.

The gravel drive behind Shelby crunched like popping corn under the weight of the firetruck. The men jumped off the vehicle and the Easy Rider, already on the porch now, kicked open the door to the house, leading the way inside.

The days were growing shorter now. The trees, proud survivors of the worst drought in Georgia state history, held tightly to their leaves, but like the days these too were changing; saturated greens giving way to yellows and plums, oranges and red. Henry raised his hand above his head, a way to shield his eyes from the dappled light playing in dancing patterns across his face, and watching as the bulldozer loaded the last pile of Marcus Hart's childhood home into the bed of a blistering red dump truck.

"That's the last of it, Marcus. Now you've got all the room

in the world for tomatoes, peppers, corn, eggplant, water-melon, whatever you please," Henry announced as if reading from a shopping list.

Marcus adjusted his baseball cap bringing the bill downward toward his nose, his own way of dealing with the sun. Gertrud sat on his foot, a behavior she'd perfected since coming home, her little chicken body emanating contentment through a series of low pitched cackles and clucks. Marcus bent down and picked her up, but when she protested, carefully returned her to the perch of his foot where she quickly settled back down, renewing the harmonious song.

"I don't think so, Henry. Turns out I'm not much of a farmer." He was referring to the pot garden he and Henry were tending on the Tate's back patio. Though none of the tomatoes or peppers had died, none had thrived in the heat and a yield of just a handful of each had sent Marcus to the farmers market twice weekly to collect the vegetables he and Lydie needed for the recipes they prepared together each night. "You're retired, why don't you farm it? I'll rest at home and keep Lydie company like you should be doing."

Henry smiled. Since his retirement, his thoughts had been taken over by an overwhelming urge to do anything *but* rest. He felt his days now as numbers, flirting, vulnerable digits straddling both sides of an invisible decimal, and he, the walker of a tightrope, performing a volatile routine whose outcome might depend on something as simple as misjudging a step or overlooking a mislaid bar of soap in the shower. When the Life Alert commercials played across the television, Henry switched channels.

When he woke in the morning his legs were the thing with

which to keep up. It seemed to Henry that these limbs acted with tenacious independence, swinging themselves over the bedside each morning before the rest of him became fully, cognitively awake. He now rushed in everything he did; to kiss his wife, to make the breakfast eggs that Gerty so generously gave, to encourage Marcus, "to get to writing that play," to his volunteer job as the outreach coordinator for at risk youth at the Macon County Boys and Girls Club. He now felt a purpose beyond the community of himself and Lydie, beyond the memory of his son, even beyond the addition of Marcus. Henry Tate, former sheriff, doting husband, heart broken father, reluctant church deacon, former sweetheart of a dead girl, had become plainly and simply, an optimist.

Glasses were beyond half full, handicapped chickens missing part of a foot could indeed live happily in a box on the sun porch and were not too much trouble to be carried around. Heartbroken men would learn to love again and write award winning plays from the kitchen table of their adopted family's home somewhere in the middle of Georgia. And women, beautiful, beloved, silver haired women could live happily after a stroke, speaking through the side of their mouths, sometimes stumbling across words, but really when you think about it, didn't we all stumble across words from time to time?

Optimism: It was Henry's religion and he, the head evangelist.

Now it was Henry who reached down and took hold of the bird. "Gerty, you good old girl, let's go. I'm too busy to stand here and watch something that once was." He slapped Marcus on the back. "Let's go home."

The chicken, once the great adventurer of her flock, put her head into the partnership of his armpit, the way she now liked to be carried as if seeing where she was going was too much of a burden to bear alone.

As the car pulled away from the gravel drive, Marcus looked back. There she was, Dorey the dead girl, waving to him from atop the mound, the place where the well had once been.

Tom Cat

Things had a way of ending up in Mrs. Krenshaw's front garden. The list to date, thus far included: one package of pastel Jordan Almonds, three maxi pads, unused and housed tightly in a festively designed Cellophane wrapper suggesting a party lying somewhere therein, three Frisbees-one "professional grade," whatever that meant- and a tire, still spinning from the accident.

So it was of little surprise to Mrs. Krenshaw when she found amongst her petunias a cat the color of the orange blossoms but not so much the pinks and it was amid those that the animal stood out.

"Puss, you're smushing my blooms. Kindly disperse."

The cat pricked up his ears but beyond that, made no other attempt at movement. Unfazed by the cat's visible disinterest, Mrs. Krenshaw went on.

"You're an animal, not a Petunia and this is a Petunia bed. Petunias being of the order *Solanaceae* and you being of the order *Felis Catus*. So go." She began the exercise of shooing the cat, gloved hands waving at the creature as if fanning an insubordinate fire. But the cat just lay there staring up at her, most likely appreciating the scientific lecture.

Next, with arms propelling wildly like that of a rudder she twirled, but still, the cat remained fixed among the flowers.

She tried stomping her feet while at the same time shouting nonsense words, original incantations such as *abooga!* and *chipmunkia!*, the crushing of the sea green grass beneath her feet the only tangible result of her enthusiasm.

Finally came the finger pointing, the cocking of the thumb, a hearty "*Bang!*," discharging her mouth as the bullet escaped the impromptu gun. Not understanding the dangers of weaponry, real or imagined, the ginger cat yawned in reflection of what he surely perceived as hijinks. Then, theatrically as cats will do, the kitty rolled over onto its back; an attempt to impress Mrs. Krenshaw by showing off a soft, round belly. It was from this vantage point that the old lady formed an assessment: The cat was fat. Lazy. Breaking her flowers from part to gather. And worst of all, still in possession of his manly parts. What she had on her hands was a tom. Profanity would be unavoidable.

"Son of a bitch. I am defeated by a pussy." Reluctantly she bent down. "Fine, I'll get you myself."

She now had the cat by the scruff of the neck. Surprisingly, he made no attempt at escape. Looking deeply into his eyes, she understood why.

Recently, on *The Google*, she had read an article concerning reincarnation and punishment and how to the Hindu, the concepts were married like a moth to a flame. At the time she hadn't given the piece much thought, but now, inspecting the cat, she did. For staring back at her were the eyes of her departed husband, Mr. Milton P. Krenshaw.

"Well, I'll be," she started, but didn't bother to finish the sentence. Neatly, she tucked Milton into the crook of her arm and took off for the house where once inside, Mrs. Krenshaw began recounting forty years worth of news, information to which Milton listened passively, his tail moving back and forth like the pendulum of a clock.

The next few hours saw to the resettling of Mr. Krenshaw. A favorite meal was prepared as well as a box where the metamorphosed could do his business. The sweet smells of success filled the house.

At dinner wine was offered in a goblet placed upon the floor, but Milton, never much of a drinker, politely refused. "Your loss, my dear," Mrs. Krenshaw declared, unable to disguise her unbridled delight as the now declared majority shareholder of the bottle. The first glass went down smoothly, methodically, as well as the second and the third. By the time the fourth pour came around, Mrs. Krenshaw thought it best to economize her time with Milton and so drank directly from the bottle. "Mm, mm!" she explained to Mr. Krenshaw, the smacking of her plum stained lips additional proof as to just how badly her husband was missing out.

Quickly, she ran to the kitchen to throw the now empty bottle into the bin designated for recycling, the importance of which she'd also learned of on, *The Google*. *What should I do with all the old wine bottles?*, she had typed into the search bar one night. That same evening she commissioned the following queries: *How far is it to the moon? How far is it to my bathroom? How far is it to White Plains, New York? Which is better, aluminum foil or plastic wrap?* And finally, *Why can't I squeeze the Charmin?*

As far as Mrs. Krenshaw could tell, there wasn't a thing in the world that could hide from the all powerful, all knowing, *The Google*. She especially appreciated the auto correct feature as some nights the exact spelling of words could be more challenging than others. Google Maps could keep her occupied for hours.

She trotted back to the living room only to find her husband retired for the night.

"Dance with me!" she insisted, pulling Milton up from a sleeping position there on the couch. For the briefest of moments he looked at her panicked and fuzzy eyed, as if woken from a pleasant dream only to find himself in the midst of an intangible nightmare completely lacking in logic or explanation; Mrs. Krenshaw, perhaps due to the high volume of wine she had consumed seemed to be lacking any ability whatsoever to accurately interpret such a look.

"You're seeing into my soul, Milton, my very soul!"

She held her husband to her chest in a staunch, suffocating pose and in a series of complicated moves, spun him around the room, dipping him twice before dropping him hard upon the floor. Surprisingly, Mr. Krenshaw did not land on his feet. Stepping on his tail during a particularity challenging series of step-ball-changes was unfortunate.

It was only when Milton screamed under the avoirdupois of her foot that Mrs. Krenshaw realized she had forgotten to put on any music at all! Finding herself in a deep, penetrating sorrow, she too fell to the floor, the regret of the moment harnessing her like a weight upon her back.

"I'm sorry, Milton. I should have played our song!" Fat tears streamed down the fault lines of her face as snot, like the albumin of an egg, slid from her nose into her open, wailing mouth. The silence of the room, so unmusical, echoed all around her, swaddling her in misery, distinct and personal; salt rubbed deep into the wound.

For a long time after she sat on the floor subconsciously humming the overlooked song, the ticking of her Aunt Lucy's grandfather clock joining in the melody, together creating a time signature she did not comprehend. Milton was nowhere to be seen.

Time passed on the floor as time does. Mrs. Krenshaw's mind drifted from the tragedy at hand to the more mundane. How much butter did she have in the fridge, had she remembered to mail the light bill, and finally, who *had* shot JR? She couldn't remember. Was it Bobby? Sue Ellen? Surely not Miss Ellie. It was all too much. She put her head in her hands. How on earth would she ever get her tired old body free from the gravitational pull of the floor? Sudden inspiration hit by way of remembering the bottle of bourbon she kept in the tank of the toilet.

She pulled herself up the best she could and made her way down the hall toward the bathroom. Milton, already haven forgiven his wife her two left feet as well as her lack of atmospheric planning, emerged from his hiding place and gracefully, jumped back onto the couch. Finding his impression still lingering atop the crushed velvet, he settled back in, the last of the uncomfortable moments erasing themselves from his mind.

The pipes screamed beneath the house, announcing the preparation of Mrs. Krenshaw's tub. Scented salts, both orange blossom and lavender, Mr. Suddzies Bubble Bath and a generous pour of the bourbon went into the elixir of her bath. As she worked the lather up and down her body she thought of Milton and where he would sleep the night away. On the couch? In a box she would stuff for him with worn out towels and seldom used doilies? In the bed, with her? But he had been gone for forty years! Was it too soon? Was she acting loose, like her forever slutty sister Gladdys? She thought not. She longed to feel her husband between her legs again. Besides, he was no longer a human, but a cat. What could be the harm in that? And perhaps even, he would purr.

Steam bound from the bathroom door and out into the hall where it faded into the thick, black spots bound to the molding, blemishes fed nightly by Mrs. Krenshaw's forgetful nature, for not once in all of her fifty plus years in the house had she turned on the vent. At times she looked upon the Rorschach like mold and imagined she saw the faces of her past; Milton's, their daughter Elizabeth who remained estranged from her even now, even after Mrs. Krenshaw had tried to make amends. Hadn't she taken to hiding her bottles in the toilet just for that reason? Hadn't she tried?

Some nights were spent entirely studying the mold. Finally, after much deliberation between herself and a team of experts, celebrity notables such as Mr. Jack Daniel and the honorable Jim Beam, a decision had been reached. The images were not of Milton, or Elizabeth, or even of her dead mother, a lovely woman whom Elizabeth in her youth had called Nonie, but that of Richard Nixon, Richard Burton and Richard Simmons, all wearing a series of constantly changing striped tank-tops and neck cravats. In the end, they all pretty much looked like sailors.

But now that Milton was back everything was changing. She knew this would be her last night with the bottle. With his return she would be strong, able to free herself of the clutter that took up so much of the thinking space in her mind. She would call Elizabeth in the morning, leave her a message on her voice mail machine. Maybe her only child would call back, maybe she wouldn't. That part was up to Elizabeth, but Mrs. Krenshaw would be "reaching out," the exact behavior Elizabeth accused her of neglecting each time they quarreled.

Maybe she would even remember to turn on the vent, sending the steam out into the night air instead of to the Richards. With Milton back, the future was wide open.

In the morning, with her husband at her side, she would place even the unopened bottles on the curb. What use would they be to her now? With the return of her beloved Milton, she didn't need them. Sure, he was a cat now, which didn't make him exactly perfect, but really, who was? From this moment forward, she would be drunk on life!

As the noxious odor of the bath wrapped her in its scent, Mrs. Krenshaw prepared to sing.

"This one goes out to you, Milton!" she cried, the sound of her voice lost before it could enter the hallway.

It's only a paper moon
hanging over a cardboard tree

But it wouldn't be make believe if you believed in me

Milton, now in full slumber on the couch, chased the butterflies drifting through his mind. A bright orb in the sky distracted him. He discontinued the hunt and following the path of its warmth, lay down in a soft place made up entirely of flowers. Their petals felt sticky, some even stuck to his fur. It was like the time he and the girl had sampled the marshmallows together, how they had stuck to his nose, how she had laughed, gently wiping them away.

Purring greeted Mrs. Krenshaw as she retrieved her husband for bed. "You remember!" she cried, bringing the cat to her chest once again and working him like a squeeze box. Milton let out a squeak, a sound reminiscent of air being forced from a ball; further conformation that he had recognized their song. So inspired by this positive response that she intended to squeeze him again, but was interrupted by a knock at the door.

Mrs. Krenshaw, still damp in her night coat dropped Milton to the floor and cautiously pulled back the curtain. There before the lace stood a small, crying girl and a man with worry written like prose among the wrinkles of his forehead. A feeling of dread fell upon Mrs. Krenshaw, but still, she opened the door. How easily the locks released themselves. How quickly Milton ran out past her, the tip of his tail brushing lithely against her leg like a feather.

The child wasted no time in scooping up the cat.

"My Tom!" she exclaimed, hugging the animal to her chest in the same suffocating way that only a moment before Mrs. Krenshaw herself had been guilty. The man grabbed Mrs.

Krenshaw's hand practically out from under her and in vigorous admiration shook it, the lines of his face now retreating
like the last bit of sun from the sky.

"No!" screamed Mrs. Krenshaw, reclaiming her hand then
the tom. "He's mine!" The cat looked from the old woman to
the girl, then back again twice more before settling his gaze
on Mrs. Krenshaw.

A new sound began to come from the cat, low, guttural,
nothing like the purr from before.

Wide eyed the girl pleaded with the man. "But daddy,
that's my cat."

The man looked to Mrs. Krenshaw, an air of astonishment
settling around the rims of his eyes. "What's wrong with you,
lady?"

"What's wrong with me?" she countered, expending zero
effort to hide her offense at the question. Hadn't she always
done the right thing when objects appeared in her garden?
Hadn't she always returned the things that she found? The
Frisbees to the children who threw them? The tire to its owner
even though she had plans for planting a raised bed in its
middle?

Hadn't she shared the almonds at church? Given the
maxi pads to the All Saints Reformation Episcopal Mexican
Women's Shelter? No sir, there was nothing wrong with her,
but there was something wrong with these two people standing on her porch. Strangers who came uninvited, knocking
in the night, foolishly mistaking her husband for the pet of a
child. Oh the indignity she suffered at their hands!

And now here was Milton struggling in her arms, the call
of the open road before him again. He'd always been so weak

when it came to the opposite sex, never any resistance to the cunning guiles of the female kind. Their pouting lips, their naked summer legs, the way their bosoms bounced as they pranced down the dairy aisle of the supermarket.

The cat dug his claws into the flesh of her arms and Mrs. Krenshaw no longer able to hold on was forced to let go. Now free, the tom cat took off down the walk, the girl and the man following closely behind.

"I forgive you, Milton!" Mrs. Krenshaw yelled out, watching helplessly as her husband left yet again with another woman.

She turned and went back in the house, shutting the door behind her. She didn't mess with the lock. What good was a locked door anyway?

The lid of the toilet felt cold against her bare bottom as she drank. There would be no bottles on the curb in the morning. No call to Elizabeth. No one between her legs tonight. Milton was gone.

She would wake in the sameness of a new day. Broken. Alone. The promise of nothing before her but of what she might find cast off, lost or mistaken, and waiting for her, there in the garden.

El Lechuguero

Shades of green.

Mantis, olive, teal, spring. Pine, sea foam, mint. Asparagus, apple. Shamrock. Chartreuse. I am all these.

"de Soto, Anthony!" The foreman reads from his list and though I am here, I cannot answer; soundless, I lie among the rows.

The crowd reminds him that it has been months since I have picked, but he ignores this, moving on to the next name on the list. *Delacruz, then Diaz, Espinoza.*

The foreman never repeats a name. If you're not there when he calls yours, someone else will take your place. *Muy mal, muy triste.*

Fernandez, Flores, Garcia. Hernandez always takes a while.

Night still holds the morning with its chill. Some try to shake it off, pulling their collars close, but others leave it alone, let it settle in, welcome it into their bones. This is the day The Lord has made. Let us rejoice and be glad in it.

Soon the truck starts up, the ancient engine sounding like a drum. *A* through *M* climb into the back, heading to a field a half-mile down the road. *N* through *Z* will stay here.

On heavy feet they come out into the rows, hands veiled by stains, swatting away invisible flies. On their heads they wear the shroud of the picker; throw-away towels tucked strategically under caps. An illusions of wings. Gently they flutter, riding the morning breeze.

The blades of their knives catch the light, so resplendent in the morning sun. For a moment I think I am seeing angels; the Lettuce Men.

Squares of brown cardboard become boxes. Like empty box cars waiting to be filled they line the rows. In the soft, green grass of a backyard they could be the imagination train of a creative child.

One by one the pickers drop to their knees, bodies yielding to work. The motion is neither fluid or rigid; so few things in life are absolute.

Soon their knives will be upon me. I will think of her while I wait. But I must be quick, the picker wastes no time.

● ● ●

Girls, my Abuela used to say, would be my downfall. "You are too pretty," she told me as I rode the horse of her knee, though at the time I didn't understand for what.

"He's a real looker alright," my grandfather would agree, kissing us both when leaving for work, me solidly on the top of the head, my grandmother on the cheek, his lips gently embracing her skin, the touch like a whisper only the two of them could hear.

When my parents died in the accident my grandfather came out of retirement to raise me, reapplying for the job in which he had spent forty-five years working in the maintenance department for the city. "Don't worry about it," my grandmother would say when I grew old enough to worry about it, "he's still a young man." He seemed ancient to me already, the age of sixty-five sounding more like a jackpot prize than an age.

The days he worked in the park close to our house we would go and watch him, my grandmother theatrically spreading a blanket across the ground; prime real-estate from which we would take in the scene of my grandfather tightening the bolts holding the swings to their chains or scrubbing the gang tags from the slides. My grandmother called this time my "training," but not for a life such as this. She was showing me what I should avoid.

"There is nothing wrong with this work," she would say as she narrated the scene before us, "all honest work honors God. But Anthony, this is work for your abuelo, not for you. You will work in an office feeding numbers into a machine or in a hospital where people will call you doctor and shake your hand because you have done something so good, *so amazing*. You will be more than we are. You will be more than this."

Sometimes my grandfather would allow me to hand him tools from his box, explaining to me the difference between a wrench and a ratchet, a hammer and a mallet. "When I grow up I want to be just like you," I would tell him, my love for this man stuck like a fist in my throat.

"No, no Anthony, this life is not for you," he would insist, every time, his words a direct echo of my grandmother's.

They were a team, the two of them, from an early age preaching me beyond the shared walls of our duplex, past Luna's market on the corner, away from the men who stood like guardians at the doors dealing out destruction, one dime bag at a time.

"Don't talk to those men, ever," my grandfather warned as we walked way around them, "They will suck you in. They have nothing for you but death."

Over the river and through the woods, the long way to grandmother's house we go.

At night, perched like an owl on the edge of bed, my grandfather would tell me stories from Mexico and Texas, which used to be Mexico, a fact of which he never failed to remind me.

"Shall we start with "The Bear Prince,"or the one about the evil wizard who kidnaps young maidens, keeping them forever a slumber, hidden deep within the secret chamber of his draconian lair?" he would ask me almost every time, his face lighting up with the possibilities.

But my favorite story, the one that I would beg for, was that of a beautiful veiled specter, killed before her time, who wandered the village graveyard wooing unsuspecting lovers deep into the ground; an attempt to satisfy both loneliness and death.

"Poor fools," my grandfather would council as the story came to its end. "Young men so blinded by love for the ghost that they never knew what hit them before it was too late. Explotar!"

The veiled specter was my grandmother's least favorite of all Grandfather's stories and whenever he recounted the tale, she insisted upon issuing a disclaimer. "Too scary, these fairy tales you tell our boy. He won't sleep a wink."

"It is good to have a warning," Grandfather would counter, turning to me. "All good stories come with a warning, Antonio. The trick, my young friend, is figuring out what the warning is before it's too late."

They found me a school a forty-five minute bus ride away. I overheard them saying that I qualified for a scholarship, if only they could make the words look right. For three nights they sat hunched together at the kitchen table, the Macramé shade covering the single bulb above their heads a victim in the path of the ever-present, oscillating fan, the fixture twisting and spinning, shadows like spider webs, connecting the four vanilla walls of the room.

On the final night of their labor my grandmother sealed her chest with the sign of the cross while my grandfather bowed his head. He cast his hands upward toward the ceiling, holding the pose; an expression he often used to signify burdens being given away.

After breakfast the next morning, the three of us walked hand-in-hand to the post office to mail the envelope, crossing the street in front of Luna's in order to avoid the men at the door. My grandparents lifted me by my arms to swing me. "You are a bird in flight!" my grandmother told me each time my feet left the ground.

At the post office I was allowed to put the envelope in the slot and when I peeked through the miniature door to route the course of the letter with my eyes, a sucker came through the narrow opening.

"Thank you!" I said, with surprise. " Candy hace de un niño dulce," came the reply.

On the way home I crushed the sucker between my teeth, gooey, sticky artificial sweetness dripping down my chin and onto the collar of my shirt. "We will shout it out!" my grandmother declared, referring to a commercial that played regularly during her afternoon shows. The sky was the limit that day. I could feel it in their arms as they held me, in their lips as they took turns planting kisses on my cheeks, even in the cadence of their steps as they danced me down the street.

"Looking good, grandma!" the guardians shouted as I flew by them. Breaking his own rule, my grandfather tipped his hat to the men. "Don't I know it!" he shouted back, my grandmother smiling wildly before begging him to stop.

That evening I sat on the edge of the bathtub watching as my grandmother shaved the stubble from his chin, my grandfather bending down low to welcome the razor, the touch of her hand.

"Always keep your face smooth for your lady Anthony, and she will reward you," he told me, winking his eye.

"Shhh," she hushed him, her face flushing red. "I will cut you on purpose." It was a promise she never kept.

My grandfather once told me that when he met my grandmother she became his guide, that from that moment forward that he knew, whatever her path, he too would go that way. "She was like the North Star and I a love sick sailor. I could not let her out of my sight. Even now, when I am away at work, I think of her, counting the hours until we are together again. A lamp unto my feet Antonio, a light unto my path."

They couldn't have loved each other any more, had they tried.

I was never alone on the bus, my grandfather arranging his work schedule so that he could accompany me in the morning, my abuela taking the afternoon shift. In was in this way that I heard their stories and though these tales were mostly communal, each teller had a slightly different version of the same events.

"She wore a yellow dress," my grandfather recalled of the day when he first laid eyes upon my grandmother. "It was green," she corrected later during the afternoon ride home. "That poor man has always been color blind."

As a list of discrepancies began to take shape, such as the name of the Corriente cow who wandered the streets of their village in Mexico or of the number of monkeys surviving the circus train derailment grew exponentially from the morning to the afternoon's version, I began to see that truth, like a mirror, could be fractured into many versions. While what was reflected in the broken pieces was identical, the portion one viewed could be conceived completely differently from that of someone else's, depending on the perspective.

The dress *was* green, a large scrap of the lace my grandmother dug out from a tomb-like box beneath their bed proved it, but the day they first met, my grandmother stood in sun, the light from that blinding star washing the color from the garment as bleach from a bottle.

The cow had no given name, though most in the village settled on Madre', taking turns milking her and sharing in the gain, while an official account of the train wreck survivors was lost to the jungle, as the monkeys released themselves into freedom much too quickly for any definite count to be tallied.

What was important was the essence of that truth; that love had happened, the cow had provided, the monkeys belonged to no one. Nothing more. When I would tell my grandfather of Abuela's corrections on the next mornings ride, he would shrug. "Well mi nieto, you get the idea."

With the turning of the buses wheels, the geography of our city unfolded as if in one of my grandfather's stories.

Once upon a time there was a neighborhood of tidy adobes guarded by metal fences. The people of this place were naturally a beautiful nut colored brown but made even more so because they worked in the sun painting benches in the parks, picking the litter from the ground or the harvest from the fields. Some said the land of adobes was a magical place where barbecue pits spit fire like dragons while beautiful senoritas danced the grass to bare clay, their bodies swaying and spinning to music escaping the open windows of cars passing by. But still, others were not so sure.

They thought the barbecue pits were nothing more than places where one could roast meat and the girls and the music were only pleasant distractions. So these people left in search of something else, and even if they didn't quite know what it was for which they were looking, they knew what it wasn't; the things they left behind.

Now these people, these explorers, were very brave because they knew that their best chances of finding what they were seeking lie somewhere in the silver city, a magnificent place of glass towers built so high that their tops cut through the sky, sometimes even piercing the clouds, slicing them into pieces so small, so insignificant that the clouds had no choice but to give up and float away.

The city was full of things that could not be so easily explained. Like a building housing nothing but books; thick, love-worn volumes thumbed through so frequently as to never gather dust. A grand palace full of paintings and beautiful objects born of clay and of precious stones brought up from the depths of the earth. And a place of noble spirit where learned people would meet and decide how to be fair, the words, 'iustitia in' carved boldly in remembrance above the doors.

Shops where people would pay an hours wage for a cup of coffee. Parks without tags. Houses without fences. Markets free of men guarding doors. Such precious things. How did they exist? How could they last?

But the most miraculous of all these was a building in which to learn, a place where a child could see his future fold out before him like the squares of a hop-scotch board each time he skipped through the door. No waving wands of a metal detector to obscure it, no pockets turned out, no arrest to be made. A place safe from all these.

This was the reason to go to the silver city, to rise early, to catch the behemoth, the great humming monster who rattled and bumped hanging sideways round corners, spewing noxious blackness as it went along. The beast would take you to paradise, show you what could be had, then return you back home to the adobes, so that you would know what never could be. A spill ride of things hoped for, but not yet fully received.

In the silver city was a girl with hair the color of straw and eyes like the sky on cloudless autumn days. When she smiled her face wore dimples, crevasses so deep that if happiness came in liquid form she could fill the wells of her cheeks again and again, never worrying the borders would be breached.

Jennie.

I sat at my desk watching as she hung her sweater among the row of hooks occupying the wall. It was the first day of school and while other parents lingered, milling about in the room bragging loudly on the abundance of books in the class library or leaning in closely, begging for a kiss, I was alone, my hands clasped tightly under the lip of my desk, my grandfather already having caught the bus back to our side of the city for work.

She turned and scanned the classroom, her gaze falling on me. Immediately, I felt panicked, cornered. To avoid the burn of her eye I concentrated on my hands, but it didn't work; within seconds she was standing in front of me.

"We're the only ones alone. Can I sit by you?"

Before I could answer she was sharing my chair, our hips crowded in an uncomfortable marriage like that of conjoined twins.

"Can I hold your hand?" she asked, reaching under the desk, unwinding my fingers to make room for her own.

I turned to face her, to study this person so freely giving herself to me. Skin so translucent that if I dared I could have mapped the river of her veins with my finger. Eyelashes the color of sifted sand, freckles scattered like thrown stars across her nose, glossy scented lips, satin hands. Glowing beauty; sun flare, raindrops, snowdrops, dew.

"Where is your mother?" she asked.

"Dead," I replied, taking my eyes from her crystal beauty. She squeezed my hand. "Mine too."

But she wasn't.

Her mother was an actress on my abuela's favorite show,

The Mirror's Edge, the soap that when it was on solicited the most begging by way of shushing; *shush, Anthony please, let me hear my show.*

Her mother played both the sweetheart and the villain, twins of polar opposite personalities separated at birth whose bitter entanglement was the driving force behind the story line of the show. As the good twin she gave birth to two beautiful children, also twin girls and as the villain she stole them only to leave the babies abandoned on the steps of an orphanage where they were taken in by a group of comely, doe-eyed nuns. But perhaps most unsettling, as the bad twin she kidnapped her better self, torturing the saintly sister by forcing her to watch a twenty-four hour video feed of the evil look-a-like making passionate love to her own, unsuspecting husband, over and over again.

During sweeps week one sister shot the other, but due to a mixed-up undercover sting operation run by the police for whom the good sister was secretly a hot shot investigator, no one knew which one was which or for whom we should root. During that time my grandmother concluded each show by drawing the sign of the cross across her chest saying that we should hope for the best but expect the worst; it was a soap opera after all.

A few days later after I'd learned the truth and asked Jennie to clarify her mistake she just shrugged. "She ignores me. As far as I'm concerned, she might as well be dead."

Jennie's fashion life played out as if she too were an actor stuck in a never ending theater piece, her clothing pulled directly from the costume closet by a clothier whose love for make-believe knew no bounds. One day she came to school dressed as Little Red Riding Hood, a long, woolen crimson cape tied neatly across her shoulders, her pink sparkly note-book and lunch box riding high in a basket swung across her arm.

On still another she played Ann of Green Gables, long braids clinging to each side of her head, her body swimming in a Calico pinafore big enough for two of her.

Cinderella at the ball, Sleeping Beauty, Gretel, they were all there, every day of the week bringing someone new. Of course, occasionally there would be repeats, for even in the world of characters, reruns are unavoidable.

But my favorite costume was that of the television char-acter, Punky Brewster. On the days that Jennie played "the Brewster," she danced into the classroom wearing striped, rainbow leggings and her favorite shoes; sequined, silver lace-ups whose soles lit up as lightning does when charging through a darkened sky.

A lamp unto my feet, a light unto my path.

And while Jennie claimed "the Brewster," as her own inven-tion, the rest she attributed to her mother's housekeeper and Jennie's full time Nannie, Rosa.

"She thinks I'm a prop," Jennie said of Rosa's desire to remake her each morning. "From one day to the next I never know who I'm going to be." In that way she lived in a constant state of anticipatory confusion, just like her dead mother the actor.

The dreamscape of her life bled over into her lunches which looked as though they had been created by a celes-tial butcher, or at the very least, craft food services. Each day when she opened her box the contents would bloom out in all directions, intricate shapes cut from a radish or fig and shaped into butterflies resting atop flowers or softly silhouetted squirrels perched upon the slender branch of a carrot stick. But in truth, these were the private creations of a sushi chef Jennie's mom kept on retainer and living in the guest cottage at the back of their property.

"Trade you for your dessert?" Jennie asked me on that first day. Never having seen food so beautiful, so delicate, I was more than happy to oblige. I put the butterfly in my pocket, a place of safe keeping until I could show my abuela on the bus ride home, but later when I pulled the creature out I found it had turned to mush, its wings crushed, unrecognizable from their time spent in the tomb of my pants.

The next day, with the intention of sharing I brought two desserts but Jennie refused, saying she would be pushing her luck to have a treat two days in a row. Her mother tested her blood for things that should not be there, traits made impossible to produce on the sushi diet alone, cells screaming of corruption from sugar or fat.

When I asked about her father she told me that he too was dead. But instead, it turned out he was a movie producer who had never married her mother and only showed up about every other year for her birthday, leading an uncooperative pony or pot bellied pig unsuited for life in the hills.

"We're not running a barnyard here, Hal," her mother would say as she turned these gifts away, a handful of the little horse's mane sliding across the top of Jennie's hand as she reached past the wall of her mother to touch the animal before it was dragged away.

We were both orphans, Jennie and I, each of us in our own

way.

After the parents left, Jennie and I went to work labeling our supplies, me writing my name, *Anthony de Soto*, in short stubby letters across folders, in text books and on handouts, while Jennie marked her possessions with only her initial paired along-side a squiggly-lined doodle of a sunflower. "Everything must be labeled," our teacher explained as she walked around the classroom checking our progress. I was so intent on claiming my property that I didn't hear Ms. Mellcamp approach and was startled to find her leaning over my desk. "I'm so glad you're here, Anthony de Soto," she whispered, but not quite in my ear.

"Me too," added Jennie, her words like a fat bumble bee stinging my chest.

By the end of that first week I had decided that Jennie and I would live together in a Lego fort that we would build ourselves. We would choose our own clothes, pets and desserts. Sugar and sweets would not be denied, blood tests of any kind were completely off limits.

I shared my plans with Jennie at recess. She was thrilled.

"Let's go ahead and get married," she said. "That way, no one can interfere. Besides, all the good equipment is taken."

She was dressed that day as Laura Ingalls Wilder, a stroke of good fortune as she was able to use her apron as a veil.

"Do you, Anthony de Soto, promise to take this woman to be your awfully wedded wife?" the fourth grader officiating the service asked.

"It's *lawfully* wedded, Andrew," the playground monitor corrected from her place on the swing where she sat checking her phone. "Lawfully," Andrew corrected. I said that I did.

"Pinky swear?" he countered. I stuck out my finger.

"And to live in a Lego fort? Even if it means you have to build it yourself because Jennie might get bored and go off and do some dumb, girl thing like play with dolls? My sister does that to me *ALL THE TIME AND IT MAKES ME SOOOO MAD!*"

I promised that under any conditions, no matter how dire, I would build that fort myself. Satisfied, Andrew turned to Jennie.

"And do you Jennie, sorry Jennie, I don't know your last name, take this man to be your *lawfully* wedded husband. To have and to hold. And some other stuff-I can't remember what else." Members of the wedding party had suggestions.

"Make Jennie say that she has to do Anthony's homework," one advised.

"And be the one that takes out the trash," proposed another. "I hate taking out the trash."

Jennie said that she would agree to have and to hold, but as far as she was concerned, that other stuff was negotiable. Andrew threw up his hands.

"Ladies and gentleman, I give you Mr. And Mrs. Anthony de Soto!" In lieu of rice the attendees threw handfuls of pea gravel gathered from around the bottom of the slide. Our heads were sore for a week.

These vows were an eight year olds equivalent of promising to love Jennie forever, to cradle her hand in mine as together we crushed the corn to make tortillas, to always bend low as she shaved the whiskers from my neck; to never mistake the color of her dress. But at the time I didn't know this. All I knew, all I understood standing on the playground that day was that I liked the touch of her skin, the secrets she whispered in my ear, the needing way she held my hand in conspiracy each day under the community of my desk.

Grandmother and Rosa became fast friends. After school, when the weather was good, they would take us to the park across the street where they would sit at a picnic table playing Conquian and gossiping about Jennie's mother and the rest of the cast on her show. Jennie and I hid in the concrete tunnels, talking about the Lego fort that I think we both knew would never actually come to fruition and practicing our kissing, hoping to perfect it to the standards Jennie's mother provided daily on *The Mirror's Edge*.

The one day my tongue accidentally slipped into her mouth, Jennie pulled away fast, wiping her lips on the sleeve of her sweater, vigorously shaking her head and telling me no, that couldn't possibly be right. Who on earth would want to kiss like that? I heard both Grandmother and Rosa yelling at us in Spanish that it was time to go home, then when we didn't budge from our lair, in English. Knowing two languages meant trouble, Jennie crawled out from the tunnel to answer the call and so I never got the chance to tell her that though it was an accident, that I would; I would like to kiss like that, very much.

I adjusted my pants, that for some reason were sticking out in front, and scrambled out after them, Grandmother grabbing my arm with one hand while waving good bye to Rosa and Jennie with the other.

"We're going to miss the bus, Anthony," she scolded.

"Sorry," I told her, but I was on auto response, the situation with my pants occupying the majority of thinking space in my mind.

Once on the bus I resumed the job of rearranging my pants. After briefly studying my predicament, my grandmother asked just what it was exactly that Jennie and I had been doing in the tunnel. Kissing, I told her. I was eight. Why would I lie? I was kissed all the time by both she and my grandfather. What was the harm in it? As far as I could see there was none.

She smiled into her reflection staring back at her from the window; on the other side of the glass the buildings zipped by like the racing story lines of Jennie's mother's show.

That evening my grandfather paid me a visit. Like most nights, he sat on the edge of my bed, but this time uncomfortably, eyes fixated on the wall opposite him, his hands busy, racing back and forth over his thighs; the fabric of his maintenance uniform going from light to dark then back again with each restless touch. He leaned in to kiss me-a smacky wet one planted firmly on my forehead- then gave me the talk. When it was over he asked if I had any questions. I shook my head, no; I certainly did not. He kissed me again then walked to the door, flipping off the light switch beside him on the wall.

"Good night, Anthony."

"Good night, Grandfather."

He closed the door behind him, leaving me in the dark.

But by middle school, I understood.

Jennie and I had taken to hiding in the janitors closet, under bleachers, behind the cafeteria dumpsters sharing space with a hundred million cigarette butts left behind by the workers. Any place where we could be alone. Stolen moments pulled from the air and made into touches, embraces, and sounds.

When were we fifteen, I laid her down across the softness of her bed. For days the strawberry smell of her hair lingered in my nose, her pleaded whispers filled my ears; *Anthony, don't ever leave me. Please, don't go.*

Somehow Rosa knew. She skipped over confronting Jennie and went straight to my Grandmother, where without conferring with my grandfather, the two Catholic ladies decided upon a plan; Rosa would take Jennie to the doctor, while my grandmother would be taking me to the priest. *Finally,* I thought, under the drunken-like influence of my newly found, manly pride, *a real confession.* I could barely wait to tell the father. I suppose I was in the mood for scandal.

On the phone that evening Jennie reported that she'd gotten the pill. I reported that I'd gotten a lecture. Celibate men sitting in little dark closets, it turned out, have little sense of humor.

When Jennie and I were seventeen, Rosa's sister who lived in San Antonio passed away. The two old ladies were now practically inseparable. To think that one could bury a sister without the help of the other was incomprehensible and so they flew out together late Friday for the Saturday service, Rosary beads in hand.

That year Jennie and I were seniors. I'd managed to keep my grades high and scholarship offers announcing my good fortune were coming in. My grandfather became the caretaker of these letters, stacking them in a intricate system of color-coded piles on the coffee table in our living room. Sometimes at night when I would sneak into the kitchen for a bowl of cereal, I would find him on his knees in front of the collection, head bowed in adjuration, hands reaching out in front of him as if the thing he prayed for could fill them with its invisible weight. I never asked him about these nights but I knew, he was praying me in the right direction, one heart-felt solicitation at a time.

I walked over to him and what had become his life's work.

"Where do you think we should go, Anthony?" he asked, sorting through the offers that had come that morning in the mail.

I leaned over to kiss the top of his head. "I don't know but I'm sure you'll figure it out. I'm going to Jennie's."

"Hey, Anthony!" he called as I was half way out the front door. "UCLA wants to know if you're, white, black, Mexican or other. I think I'll put other. Write in something creative. Maybe tell them you're a little green man from Mars!" He laughed out loud, so pleased with the joke.

"You do that Tata, knock yourself out!" I yelled, the door shutting softly behind me.

I found Jennie in the pool, her butt stuck deep into the middle of a donut shaped floaty, legs sticking out and kicking awkwardly at a fly determined to invoke squatters rights on the top of her freckled knee. I took off my shirt and jumped in, rippling streams spreading out behind me, marking the spot of intrusion on the glass-like surface of the water. My intention was to swim up beside her, to hum the *Jaws* theme, loudly, ludicrously!, dump her from the raft, make love to her in the water. But before I could put my superior plan into action, she lifted her sunglasses to the top of her head and gave me a look that read loud and clear, *no,* no to all of it.

"Guess whose mother flew in from New York this morning on the Red Eye?"

"Really?" I asked, taking hold of the raft. "No shit?"

"No shit." She pulled her glasses back down over her eyes then helped me up. I put my arms around her, kissing her long on the mouth.

Together we floated wrapped in each other's arms, the Santa Ana's pushing us around the pool in an unscripted drift. After a while, Jennie raised her head from my chest.

"We've got to decide where we're going. Rosa is driving me nuts."

I ran the back of my hand over her arm, static electricity pulling the fine, blond hairs upward in the direction of my stroke. "You name it, we'll go."

"Berkley?"

"Berkley, not Stanford?"

She thought for a minute.

"Yea, let's be hippies. Rosa can tie-die all my shirts; she'll love it."

"Good enough for me."

She returned her head to my chest. Thunder exploded somewhere on the hills behind us. *Heat lightning,* I speculated. She nodded, letting her hand drift over the edge of the inner tube and into the water.

"And anyway, I started my period this morning," she said, getting back to the reasons why we would not be having sex in the pool or anywhere else for that matter. Girl's periods were not something you messed with in high school, even if you messed with everything else.

That night when I got home I found my grandfather on the floor, one hand strung to his heart, the other clutching a welcome letter from the University of Southern Cal. He had been that way for hours, the ambulance men said with the competence brought on only by professional wisdom. They had trouble, getting him into the bag, wrestling the letter from his hand, straighting out his curled up legs.

The line to Texas hummed with the static of a thousand miles, but still not enough distance to stifle the sound of my grandmother's crying, to disguise the agonizing loss I could hear in her voice.

She and Rosa flew home that night on updated tickets purchased on a credit card that Jennie's mother had entrusted to her for such emergencies. "We will pay her back," Rosa said of the borrowing, though in the end Jennie's mother wouldn't allow it. By Monday, together the two friends had buried another love. Heartache became the new Tuesday, Wednesday, Thursday; all of the days of the week.

My grandfather began to disappear from our house in pieces. It seemed that each morning when I would wake something else would be gone; his clothes from the closet, the shaving set from beside the bathroom sink, his retirement picture from the wall. I never asked my grandmother where she put these things, but I hoped that she kept them, perhaps storing them in the museum she housed under their bed, the scrap of green lace finding itself among friends.

Eventually my grandmother lost her zest for life. She gave up cooking, soap operas, cards with the neighbors; gossip with Rosa in person and over the phone. She rarely left her spot, a worn chair of velvet sitting close to the window overlooking our now overgrown garden. From this station she watched, waiting for a man who would not return.

She quit sleeping, her eating became sporadic like that of a fickle child. I worried, fussing over her like the mother hen she had always been to me.

I will brave the jungle of our garden to pick the corn. Together WE will make the tortillas. Grandfather would be happy to know that I am taking care of you. You have taken care of me, now let me take care of you.

I have loved him so much, for so long....

I love you, Grandmother. I am still here.

...I do not know another way to live, Anthony.

You are the only mother I have ever known.

Your mother would have been so proud. She is in Heaven with your Grandfather while I am here in this box, the lid shut tight.

My grandmother, the capacity of her heart so enormous, made that way from the love she held for my Grandfather and now that he was gone she sat gaping, hollowed out. A corpse in the window, a statue in a lonely temple; the only thing left behind.

By July my Grandmother and I had settled into a comfortable routine. She insisted that I ignore the fact that she was wasting away and that we talk only of happy things, like when Mr. Menendez won three thousand dollars in the scratch off, or of our neighbor, Yolanda Esponoza, whose daughter had come in second in the county wide spelling bee, a good enough finish to send her to the state competition.

But her favorite, happy topic was of me leaving for college. For the first time in months she showed a certain kind of reluctant joy in what I thought of as un-nesting. The week before Jennie and I were to leave my grandmother busied herself embroidering my name onto the back of each and every pair of my underwear, claiming that she had heard from Loretta Campos down at Luna's that people in college would steal your drawers right out from under you. While I questioned the validity of this claim, I kept my thoughts to myself, assuming there to be worse fates than going through my freshman year of college with my underwear reading, *Property of Antonio, "Anthony," Marquis de' Soto.*

After she finished the underwear she washed and ironed all my shirts, my jeans, even my socks. She spread dried lavender in the wide, satin pocket of the suitcase I would be carrying to relieve it of its musty scent accumulated from years of time spent in storage under my bed. She filled a notebook with detailed instructions written in both English and Spanish on how to do everyday household jobs, chores such as laundry-never mix the lights with the darks-and how to heat up leftovers in a microwave. These were things that I already knew, but again, I kept my mouth shut, letting her enjoy this new comfort she had found in my leaving.

Next she packed up my room, putting everything she thought I would need into clearly labeled boxes; music, family photographs, my high school yearbooks, the rap posters from my walls. Like my grandfather she was removing me in pieces, small chunks of the things I had become, the things she thought I would need in order to continue being me.

The morning of my departure we stood on the stoop, me, soliciting promises, my grandmother engaging in a tiring game of deflection.

"You will eat, you will take care of yourself, you will do all these things for me. Promise me. Promise me now."

"Oh mi nieto, you worry much too much."

"Promise. Promise me now."

"Te lo prometo. I promise."

Satisfied, I kissed her on the cheek.

"Remember who you are, Anthony!" she yelled as Rosa's car pulled away from the curb. I promised that I would. If there was ever any question, I would only have to read the back of my underwear.

I wanted college to be a place where the color of people's skin ran together, for this blending to act as a cleansing, erasing away the years in which mine and Jennie's coupling had forced us into the spotlight in our own neighborhoods and in the social circle of Jennie's mother where when introduced to friends, I was treated as a bit of an anomaly; a Mexican whose achievements put me in a category of having a future like that of their own, my very existence dispelling the wildly held belief that my people could only watch after *their* children, keep *their* houses clean, mow *their* lawns, pick *their* fields.

Jennie hadn't fared much better in my neighborhood where she was treated as a thief, just another spoiled white girl used to getting everything she wanted and in doing so, taking away a good Mexican man from his community as well as robbing a perfectly fine Mexican girl from the pleasure of holy matrimony to me, the outstandingly good Mexican man whose value went up each time the situation was re-examined.

I believed, based on nothing but my own naive hopes, that university life would be different, that in a place of enlightenment, thinking would be enlightened as well.

But in truth, university life was about the same. In the classrooms I was treated with the same reverence to which I'd become accustomed during my earlier education, my professors taking time to ask me about my past, my plans for the future; salt and pepper heads bowing deeply, intently, as I spoke of my interest in maintaining biodiversity among genetically engineered crops or of my concern over the disappearance of the honey bee.

But when night fell and the parties happened, I would read the lips of the guys keeping watch over the keg, hitting on my girl as she topped off her glass, these wanna-be contenders looking my way in total disbelief each time Jennie pointed me out as her boyfriend.

That Mexican dude?

His name is Anthony.

Are you kidding me? That guy, really?

Silence. Cold stare.

Girl, have you looked in the mirror lately, cause you too fine. Way too fine. You should be with me.

Together Jennie and I filled out the playbill from "Beauty and the Beast," "The Frog King"; "The Bear Prince." But while the protagonist in these stories would eventually break free from the dark magic that bound them, I could not. It was as if I was cast under a spell of Mexicanism, a cruel fate for which there was no known antidote.

By the middle of our sophomore year Jennie and I had declared majors, me, agri bioengineering, and Jennie, costume design. All those years playing Rosa's doll had left an impression. When asked about the origins of her talents in fashioning hats from the Rococo era or of shaping freshly cut cane into a vertugado, she would attribute her abilities to her chosen mother, a great and famous costumer who once dressed the stars of the Palacio De Bellas Artes in Mexico city, but who when came to this country, could find work only as a domestic. She and Rosa would spend hours on the phone each week discussing the hemline of a Victorian dress or the subtle nuances distinguishing true Tudor costuming.

While our days were occupied by our studies, our nights belonged to each other. Together, we spent them crammed happily in a single size bed making love between the interruptions of room mates. When the time for sleep came, I would tell Jennie the bedtime stories of my childhood. Like mine, her favorite was, "The Lady in the Veil."

"But why didn't he know she was a ghost?" Jennie would ask me over and over like a child hearing the story for the first time.

"Because she wore a veil."

"Then how could he tell she was beautiful?"

"Maybe it was see through? Or gauzy?"

Sometimes she would talk in her sleep, I think inventing the disguise, asking an invisible assistant for a certain bolt of fabric.

No, No. The gossamer black that twinkles like star shine. The one on whose length runs the silver thread like a winding river.

I called my Grandmother every day. She would tell me nothing of herself, instead insisting that I give her every possible detail of my life at school; what I'd eaten that day for lunch, who had said what in class, what the lettuce fields that served as the lab for my genetics class looked like up close.

"It is an ocean of green. You cannot imagine, Abuela. Green as far as the eye can see. And then there are the dirt rows, breaking it up with their brown. If it weren't for the rows I might forget that I was in a field at all."

"Tell me of the sky, Anthony."

"It is so blue, blue like nothing I have ever seen and it goes on forever. Someday there are clouds of course, but somehow they only make it look bluer.

"And what of those clouds, mi nieto?"

"They are silver, Grandmother, and inside their depth hides the rain. When the clouds can no longer hold on they must let go and water pounds the earth and everyone rejoices because it is a day without irrigation. But if it rains too much, that is a bad thing too. Too much rain will melt the lettuce to nothing. It dissolves like cotton candy under a tongue. Do you remember the cotton candy you and Grandfather bought me at the carnival? How it dyed my mouth pink? How I ate it all and became ill?"

"Of course, Anthony. I would never forget. Will too much rain bring the slugs?"

"Yes, they are the beasts of the field and they are ruthless."

"What will happen, Anthony?"

"I will design a better crop. A crop immutable, unhampered by these burdens."

I now see that I was telling her stories. Fairy tales like the ones once told to me. To please her, I would end each tale with the promise of a happy ending.

"I will be the one to alter the genes of the lettuce, taking the strongest bits and pieces from many kinds. Their colors will blend into one and I will be known as the scientist who saved the crop. They will call me, The Lettuce Man."

"El Lechuguero," she would repeat wistfully, as if remembering a pleasant dream. "I will sew it into your underwear." It was the only joke she ever allowed herself.

The one thing she never asked me about were the men working the fields, their hunched over frames, picking sacks swinging from their backs as if cursed with an extra appendage. I was glad for this because in truth had she inquired, I wouldn't have known what to tell her. Would I have told her that I hated to see these men? That the permanent curvature of their spines made me view them as monsters, unwanted characters cast from one of my grandfather's tales. That their very presence brought out in me a dangerous pride that quickly gave way to a fastidious guilt. Why them and not me? Hadn't they been raised by families who loved them well, sacrificed for them, told them they were too special to work in this way? Didn't someone want better for these children now grown into men?

At times my shame was astonishing-my people, stooping over the rows-as I stood tall among them in my pressed khakis, anemometer in hand, measuring the wind; a gusting and indifferent presence. Pride, guilt, shame; invisible forces like the wind of whose effects can only be seen. No, better that she not ask. Best not to give myself away.

"You are making me so proud, Anthony. My grandson, the scientist. This is my dream coming true." She finished every conversation in this way.

The day she did not answer the phone, I knew. I asked Mrs. Esponoza to use her key, to open the door and go inside, to call out my grandmother's name, but I knew, she would be checking on the dead.

"Oh, Anthony," she cried into the phone. "Oh, baby no."

Time passes very slowly in these moments. The way Mrs. Esponoza expelled her breath, the way I held mine, the way the sirens wailed over the wire connecting the two separate places, and me, looking out my own window for the approach of the ambulance as if I were in the room waiting there with Mrs. Esponoza, seeing the thing that she saw; my abuela hanging in the window, her face veiled by the piece of green lace from the ancient dress, the velvet chair resting on its side.

Death comes for all of us. It watches us from the doorways, sneaks past our locked gates. It opens windows and climbs right through, letting itself inside. Death holds the knife, or shapes the noose, or shoots the gun. Death reaches under the bed then hands you the veil. Death makes sure the curtain rod will hold. Death kicks back the chair.

I mourned my grandmother wherever I went: the class-room, the grocery store, to bed with Jennie. But it was only in the field that I could see her. There she stood among the rows, the veil of lace spread across her face, the edges waving in the breeze like the flag of the surrendered. It was in this way that I knew her soul was wandering and that the peace that we all tell ourselves comes along side death was nothing more than an illusion; the comfort talk of those left behind.

I began skipping class, telling my professors that there was a measurement that should not wait to be taken out in the field or of a reading that could only be interpreted among the rows. But in truth I did nothing but watch the way my grandmother weaved among the workers, their seasoned hands picking right through her, scattering the thing she had become into a million tiny pieces like morning breaks apart the night.

When one field was picked my abuela would flee to the next and at a safe distance I would follow, both hoping and fearing that she would somehow be able to reach beyond the borders of her spiritual state, perhaps laying a tender hand upon my face or speaking my full name as was her custom when introducing me to a stranger. But she never did. I felt a fool, alone in my isolation and standing on the sidelines, watching a phantom whom no one else could see.

After a while the foreman stopped calling me, *"college boy"* and put a knife in my hand. "You might as well pick. I'm sick of you just hanging around," he barked, the assessment so persuasive that I had no problem adopting it as my own.

I joined in the line, holding the knife in the way that I'd learned from long months of watching the pickers. With one clean sweep of the instrument, I separated the head from the stalk, the lettuce falling unceremoniously to the ground. The man beside me nodded his head in approval. " We 're all the same now, bro," he told me, before moving on to the next row.

"I'm leaving school."

Jennie sat at the foot of the bed picking at a thread hanging from the cuff of her jeans, her long hair braided and framing both sides of her face, as if she were still eight and cast as Ann of Green Gables.

I expected a lecture. Jennie telling me that I was letting my grandparents down, reminding me that they had worked so hard, sacrificed so much, that it was my grandmother's dream for me to become a scientist. That I was not to be like them, never to work with my hands. That more than anything in the world they had wanted it that way, but those words did not come.

I studied her fingers. The way she twirled the loose thread up tightly, bringing it just to the breaking point, fingers strangled and squeezed into redness, at the last moment letting it go only to start the whole process over again.

"I feel like I'm losing you," she whispered so quietly, as if it were a thing I should not know.

At first I thought the effect was a trick of the light working its way through the shadow of the silver clouds or of the bleeding pigment of the scored lettuce seeping through the skin of my gloves. But the color went beyond my hands, traveling up onto my arms, saturating the muscles there in the deep green hues of the field. The next day my neck joined in on this, the day after my legs. My feet, my face, all places in between.

"You don't look so good," the foreman told me. "You've got an allergy. Or something."

"I'm fine," I assured him,, wedging myself down into the bed of the truck between the water cooler and a picker whose capped, golden teeth radiated in the reflection of the rising sun.

"Man, what's wrong with your face?" he asked me. "You're all green, hermano."

"Nothing brother, what's wrong with yours?"

His eyes betrayed him; fear, confusion, anger.

At the end of the day the whistle is blown. Backs are stretched, necks rolled from side to side, knives returned to sheaths; all but one. Feet planted firmly between the rows he waits for me, blocking the path to the truck. I am forced to bump past him. It is the only permission he needs.

"Hey, jolly green giant, you think you're better than me? You're no better than me."

He has moved beyond anger settling comfortably on intimidation, his once lustrous smile now extinguished by the setting of the sun.

"Hey, I'm talking to you, you green fuck."

Now the path is flooded with workers. I fall in line, walking within the sea of them. We are as shadows moving in singular drifts, overtaking, being overtaken, merging into giants destined to split apart all over again.

I feel before I hear, the knife so quiet, so surreptitious, there is no announcement of its intrusion as it enters my back.

From behind me there is commotion; my attacker being wrestled away. I hear a rushing of water, like a groundswell it rises up filling my ears. It is the blade letting loose within my heart.

My rescuers whisper. I can feel them, their eyes across my back.

It can't be.

He is bleeding green.

Lechuguero.

I am on the ground now, the rows of naked stalks surrounding me like a tomb. Someone lifts me, cradling my head between two tender hands. The touch is like ice, injected directly into my bones.

"I have been waiting for you, Anthony. Come home with me, come home with me now."

It is only now that I understand the warning, feeling its full weight upon my back. *Girls would be my downfall.* If only I had known which one.

Death comes for all of us. It climbs up onto the truck, watches from behind the rows, whispers in your ear. Death holds the knife, steadies the hand, drives the blade into the heart.

As I pull away my grandmother fades from sight. The field begins to pulse, to thump as if the land beneath me has a heart all of its own. I am changing, from solid to liquid, my flesh, my bones, my blood dissolving, oozing and seeping; the melting point of this metamorphosis beyond my control.

Mother earth embraces me, welcomes me, soothes me. Like countless others before me, I surrender myself to the ground. Now, I am home.
• • •

The pickers are getting closer. I can hear them, telling the story now.

"They say that on a full moon you can see him, a restless spirit wandering the rows."

"Bullshit. You're just trying to scare me."

"No bro, it's true. I knew him. He was a college boy, a scientist. He used to come out here and take readings and samples and all kinds of shit. Said he was working on a better kind of lettuce, something that could hold up to drought and stuff. Then one day he just went crazy and quit going to school. Nobody knows why, man. Anyway, he started picking and he had some sort of freaky reaction to the tannins or something and he turned verde.

"Green? Now I know you're lying."

"I'm not lying, I saw him myself. And then, he went and pissed off the wrong tipo-dude stabbed him in the back-knife went clean through the heart, came out the other side and everything. Blood everywhere, but here's the crazy part. It was green! His freakin' blood was green!"

"No way, man. For real?"

"For real."

Their knives surround me, slices falling upon my arms, my legs, my back. This kill will happen a thousand times over because I choose it. With their blades I am one of them, moving after each harvest through the rows of the field to fall again under the spell of their hands. There is magic in the touch of my people, beauty and warmth, joy in their laughter.

"So why does he wander, man? What's keeping him here?"

"No one knows, but if I had my guess, I'd say it's because of you."

"Me? What do you mean, bro?"

"Just look at you, hermano. Dude's obviously hot for you."

"Could be. Your sister is."

"Okay, man."

"And your mother."

"Seriously dude, shut up."

I am El Lechuguero.

I have satisfied them all.

How the Dung Beetle uses the Milky Way to Navigate the Universe

Mother and Father are getting a divorce. They have brought me here to Doctor Tanglewood so that she can tell me.

"Do you understand what I'm telling you, Isaac?"

I say that I do.

"Tell me," she insists.

"Mother and Father are getting a divorce. A divorce is a legal agreement to end a marriage. I will live with Mother in the apartment here, in Brooklyn. I will see Father three days a week. He is free to visit any time that he wants, but he must call first, and twenty-four hours ahead of time. Father will live in Brooklyn also, in an apartment that he has yet to rent. Now, can I tell you how the Dung beetle uses The Milky Way to navigate the universe?"

Mother and Father are making their unhappy faces. Doctor Tanglewood reminds them that my detachment stems from my Autism. Mother says that is bullshit, that I get my lack of sensitivity from my father. Father laughs. Now his face has changed from unhappy to happy. He uses his happy face more than Mother. Doctor Tanglewood's face stays the same, neither happy *or* unhappy.

The alarm on my watch goes off. "Times up," I say. I allow exactly four pulses to sound before I push in the button that disarms the bell. "Don't forget your coat," I tell Father. Often, he leaves his coat behind.

Our coats are hanging on the coat rack by the door. The coat rack is old and Victorian in style, with the image of a sea serpent carved along the top. Doctor Tanglewood says that the coat rack is actually called a *hall tree* and is made from Rosewood. Rosewood belongs to the genus *Dalbergia* and is primarily from Brazil.

Beneath the sea serpent carving is a row of three hooks. The hooks are made from bronze. Bronze is an alloy made from copper and tin. An alloy is a mixture of two or more metals. Copper is a chemical element listed in the twenty-ninth position on the periodic table. Tin is also a chemical element, but it is listed at number fifty on the chart.

Doctor Tanglewood is my Applied Behavioral Therapist.

The hanging order of our coats is this: Mother's on the left *or* first hook, Father's on the middle *or* second hook, mine on the right *or* third hook, which also is the last hook when counting from left to right.

My coat is white and puffy, like a Cumulus cloud, which is why I like it. When I first saw my Cumulus cloud coat in the store, it was zipped up tight from top to bottom and hanging on a hanger; fourth from the front of the rack but fifth from the back. Nine coats total. I do not ever want my coat to become unzipped so Mother has to help me get it on and off, pushing and pulling it over my head like a shirt.

As we leave, Cathy, Dr. Tanglewood's receptionist tells me, *see you later alligator*. This is a joke. I am not really an alligator. An alligator is a Crocodilian in the genus *Alligator* of the family *Alligatoridae*. I am a human being, a hominid; a creature closely related to apes. Cathy taught me to say, *in a while crocodile*. That is my part of the joke in the game that we play.

"Alligators can live to be eighty years old. Alligators can grow to be nineteen feet long," I tell Mother and Father as they push me out into the hall.

"See you same time tomorrow," Cathy calls through the door. Cathy is not a crocodile. Like me, Cathy is a human being.

"Alligators live in the Southeastern region of the United States. This includes Florida, Louisiana, the southern tip of Arkansas..."

"Want to push the down button, sport?" Father asks me. I am not a sport either; this is another joke. A sport is an activity requiring physical skill and can include basketball, football, hockey, swimming, skiing, tight rope walking, pancake making, hot dog eating.

"Not *all* the buttons, Isaac. Geez," Mother says. I have pushed all the buttons. Numbers one through thirty-six light up in their circular cases.

"Georgia, Alabama, South Carolina...."

"Okay, Isaac."

"North Carolina...."

"We know, Isaac."

"Eastern Texas, Mississippi...."

"Could you start over, Isaac?" Father asks. "I don't think I heard the first three."

"I'm going to *fucking* kill you, Rob," Mother tells Father.

"Florida, Louisiana, the southern tip of Arkansas..."

The elevator stops. A chime sounds and the doors open; the *twenty-four* button lights up. A woman standing in the door ask if the elevator is going up or down. Father tells her that yes, it surely is.

"Georgia, Alabama, South Carolina..."

The woman is holding a dog. The dog is small and white and has curly fur. The dog is barking. The dog is making its excited face. The elevator chime is stuck. *Ding, ding, ding.* I count the bells.

"One, two, three, four, five, six..."

"Are you getting on the elevator or not?" Mother uses her screaming voice, *and* makes her angry face at the woman. The woman makes her scared face.

"Ten, eleven, twelve, thirteen...."

"Push the *close door* button, Isaac," Father tells me.

I push the button. The doors come together tightly. The chime ends. The elevator lurches upward.

"North Carolina, eastern Texas, Mississippi...."

Out on the street Mother hails a cab for herself. Father and I watch as she drives away. Together, we walk the fourteen blocks back to the apartment. Father says that it is way too nice an evening to be stuck in a smelly old cab, anyway.

"Alligators lay eggs. The sex of the baby alligator inside the egg is determined by the temperature of the air surrounding the egg. Each baby alligator has an egg tooth. Each baby alligator breaks out of the egg with the egg tooth."

"Is that so?" Father asks, as we make our way home.

I do not know why Father cannot remember any of this. I have told him about the egg tooth exactly one hundred and three times and each time, he acts like it is the first.

When we get to the apartment mother is gone. She has left a note on the table. The note reads:

Call when you're finished packing and I'll come back. Make sure Isaac eats.

Father makes me chicken noodle soup and I eat it out of the red bowl. In the soup I crumble four, square crackers. I eat one canned peach for dessert. Father sits at the table and watches me. After a while he says, "I'm sure gonna miss you, buddy." He pulls me over to him and holds me tight.

"I am suffocating!" I tell him.

Father lets me go. He is making his sad face. Dr. Tanglewood has taught me that when someone makes a sad face on the outside, it is because they are sad on the inside. And when that happens, it is my job to try and understand why that person is sad. I am supposed to ask myself, *is it something I have done?* And if it is, I am supposed to wonder, *how can I fix this?*

I told Father he was suffocating me, then he became sad. Father is sad because he wants to suffocate me. If *not* getting to suffocate me makes Father sad, then *getting* to suffocate me would make Father happy.

"Okay, you can suffocate me," I tell him.

He puts his arms around me again and cries onto my shoulder. With my fingertip I push the leftover noodles around in my bowl, arranging them into concentric circles. We sit like that for a long time, suffocating and making circles.

Sometimes I wish that Doctor Tanglewood had not taught me to understand peoples faces quite so well.

The next day it snows. Mother looks out the window and makes her sad face.

"I wish we were in Florida with the alligators," she says. "Don't start!" she tells me, just as I was about to tell her about the egg tooth.

Mother is from Florida. She grew up next to an orange grove, stealing oranges when the farmer went to bed. She steals oranges here, in Brooklyn now, but from the farmers market on Atlantic Avenue. She got caught one time and told the policeman that she was sorry, but she couldn't help herself. The policeman let Mother go after she promised never to do it again, then we walked home the long way, her pockets bulging with oranges. Later that morning, she cried into the breakfast she was cooking. "My God, I fucking hate it here," she said to the eggs.

Father says that Mother never not got accustomed to the cold here and that in the winter, she turns into a snowman. That is another joke. She does not turn into a snowman, but she is very cold. He also says that Mother, even though she is not a native New Yorker, will make it here anyway because she is so good at cursing. Her favorite curse work is *fuck*.

Fuck you, Rob. Go die for all I fucking care.

Fuck you, mother fucker.

Fucking Hell! Fuck-ing Hell!

What the fuck? Fuck!

Dr. Tanglewood says that Mother is a very interesting person, linguistically speaking.

"Time to rise and shine," Mother tells me, handing me my clothes. "Today, on your bottom, you will be wearing Levi's 501 jeans over your spaceship underwear. On your top you will wear a long sleeved t-shirt with a logo reading, *NYU Space Camp*. Over the t-shirt, you will wear a sweater. The knit of the sweater is called "Fisherman's." The jeans are blue, the t-shirt is black, the sweater is green. Okay?"

"Okay," I tell her, "but what about my feet?"

"How about for your feet you decide?"

"No thank you." It is my job not to scream "no" until after I have said "no thank you."

"Isaac..."

"No, no, no! You decide for my feet! You do it! You!"

Mother looks out the window at the snow again. "Those alligators are sounding better all the time."

On the way to school we talk about Father.

"How did he seem last night?" Mother wants to know, then corrects herself when she sees that I am making my confused face. "I mean, what did your Father do last night? And, what did you do?"

"He made his sad face so I let him suffocate me."

Mother squats down in front of me and brushes the hair out of my eyes. "That was very nice of you, Isaac," she says, before kissing me on the cheek.

Kissing me on the cheek is now okay since I have graduated from that class at school.

School goes like this: First, occupational therapy.

Mrs. Cardamom is my therapist. Things I know about Mrs. Cardamom:

Her skin is brown.

She speaks with an accent.

She chews gum. Spearmint is her favorite flavor.

She has three earrings in each ear.

She keeps her cell phone clipped to her belt.

Her teeth are big and stick out when she smiles.

I think Mrs. Cardamom is beautiful. Like a circuit tester.

"What should we do today, Isaac? Jump some rope?"she asks.

"No thank you."

"What about the balance beam?"

"No thank you."

"Play a little catch?"

"Yes. Play a little catch!"

"You choose the ball, Isaac. Remember, like you did the last time? You were very good at choosing the ball the last time we played."

The problem with choosing the ball is that there are so many choices. In the bin to the right of the window, there is one red ball, one blue ball, and one green ball. In the bin to the left of the window, there is one yellow ball, one orange ball, and one rainbow colored ball. I hate the rainbow colored ball; it confuses my eyes.

"Go ahead, Isaac. You did it before, you can do it again," Mrs. Cardamom tells me. Her big teeth stick out from between her lips; I can see the tip of her tongue. The average human tongue has between three and ten thousand taste buds on its surface.

I walk over to the balls. When I touch the red ball, it burns my hands. When I look at the rainbow colored ball, my stomach feels sick. The yellow ball is too bright; the orange ball makes me sad. It is between the blue ball and the green ball. Quickly, I choose blue ball before the green ball has a chance to get angry.

"Blue. Nice choice, Isaac!" Mrs. Cardamom tells me. "Now, show me those catch hands."

I position my arms straight out in front of me. "Ready Mrs. Cardamom!" I shout. I close my eyes in anticipation of the ball, but Mrs. Cardamom tells me that I must keep my eyes open.

"One!" I yell, as the ball hits me in the face.

"Try again!" Mrs. Cardamom tells me and we do, nineteen more times. My nose is sore by the end.

We finish our session together with scissor therapy. By the end of the morning I can almost cut a straight line down the middle of a piece of wide-ruled paper. Mrs. Cardamom tells me that I am doing a very good job remembering which hole is for my thumb and which hole is for my fingers.

Second: Lunch.

This is what I eat everyday: Four slices of soy turkey, rolled around one slice of American cheese; one long, dill pickle hiding in the middle. Six carrot sticks. One apple, green. One carton milk; two-percent.

Third: Learning.

I am in a class with two other students; Rose and Michael. Rose's last name is Fernanda and Michael's is I do not know. When I get to class Rose is already busy counting the electrical outlets in the room. Sometimes we count them together, but usually, she has them all counted by the time I get to the classroom.

"Hi, Rose," I tell her. It is our job to greet each other by name, everyday. If we forget, we have to leave the classroom, come back in and try again.

"Hi, Isaac," she tells me, but doesn't look up from her counting. "There are no new outlets today. No new outlets, Isaac. Nothing new. Twelve outlets. Twelve."

I walk past Rose to see what's on the *Exploration Table!*. Michael is already there, going through the items. Today, on the *Exploration Table!*, we have: two AM/FM clock radios-no brand names showing, one toaster oven-Black and Decker brand, one compact disc marked, "Piano Classics," one musical keyboard-Casio brand, one *Build it yourself Marble Shoot*, one box of forty marbles-assorted colors including rainbow. But because the marbles are also partially white, they do not make my stomach hurt.

"Hi, Michael," I tell him. He is holding the classroom compact disc player to his chest.

"Hi, Isaac," He tells me back, in his usual whisper. Michael only speaks in a whisper and sometimes it is hard to hear him over Rose's screaming. Rose screams *a lot*. "Do you have your screwdriver with you today, Isaac?"

"No," I whisper back. "I left my screwdriver at home, sitting beside my circuit tester."

"Where are they? Where did you leave them?"

"In my room, on my dresser; six inches from the window, five feet from the closet door. The closet door is comprised of six panels of wood; the panels are painted. The color of the paint is called *Lantern Mist* and is made by the Benjamin Moore paint company. The Benjamin Moore paint company was established in 1883."

"*Yes,*" Michael whispers, "*Yes.*" I think I am making Michael happy but I can never really tell because his face never moves.

Mr. Sheldon is our teacher. He tells us that we have thirty minutes to work on the computer, so please sit down in front of a computer. *Now please*. And that our word to research is *music*.

"Now, when you type the word, *music*, into the search bar, you will have many choices to click on. I know that having many choices can be overwhelming. So, Rose, you pick the first link that comes up. Michael, you pick the second and Isaac, you pick the third. Wear your headphones, explore your link, have fun."

I sit at the computer station between Rose and Michael. Rose sits on my left, Michael sits on my right. There are one hundred and four keys on the computer keyboard. I type in, M U S I C.

First link: *Music* on Wikipedia. That one is for Rose. Second link: *Music* on eTunes. That link is for Michael. Third link; *Music* on **The Top Ten Classical Piano Pieces of All Time**. That one is for me. I move the arrow until it rest on top of the words, then I click down on the mouse. These are the words that I first see on the page; "Claire de Lune," *and* "Liebestraum

Number three in E Flat." Further down I read; *click to hear a sample*. When I do, my headphones fill my ears with sound.

When the thirty minutes is over, Mr. Sheldon has us sit in a circle on the floor facing each other. He starts with Rose.

"Rose, please tell our group what you learned about music."

"Okay," Rose says while looking up at the light fixture hanging above our heads. I look too. Four light bulbs, two filaments in each bulb; eight filaments all together.

"Can you please look at your friends, Rose?" Mr. Sheldon says that.

"Okay." Rose stretches the skin around her eyes wide open with her fingers. "Okay. Okay. Okay," she says, turning her face from Michael to me. "Music sounds."

"Very good, Rose. What else?" Mr. Sheldon, again.

"Dunno."

"Very nice, Rose, thank you. Michael," Mr. Sheldon now turns to Michael, "what did you learn about music?"

Michael is sitting on his hands, rocking back and forth in what Mrs. Cardamom would describe as a 'fast pace.'

"It's a secret," Michael whispers.

"No, no it isn't, Micheal, please stop rocking back and forth. Take your hands out from beneath you. We'll have personal time in a few minutes." Micheal takes his hands out from beneath him and sits up very, very straight. "I'm ready," he whispers.

"Great, then go ahead, Michael, we're ready too."

"eTunes is your number one music source. We have everything, from Hip-Hop to classic, R&B to metal. Grammy award winners, pop stars, country crooners, opera divas; get it all on eTunes. Click here for a free demonstration. Then, I clicked."

"Can you speak up a little, Michael?" Mr. Sheldon wants to know.

"No," Michael tells him.

"And what happened when you clicked on the free demonstration button?"

"It's a secret."

"No, it isn't, Michael. We're all your friends here and we don't have secrets. Rose, don't you want to hear what happened when Michael clicked on the free demonstration button?"

"No thank you, Mr. Sheldon. No thank you. No thanks."

"Thank *you,* Rose for saying, *no thank you.* Michael, did *you* hear some sounds?"

"Yes."

"Could you sing what you heard? Singing is a way to make music."

Michael nods his head and whispers, "Okay."

"Please, go ahead, Michael."

Michael slides his hands back under his bottom and resumes rocking. In his whispery voice he says:

> *Morning time on the table, night time in the bed*
> *makin' love to you Mabel, is my greatest love and dread*
> *Cause when I'm with you Mabel,*
> *strange thoughts go through my head*
> *Morning time on the table, night time in the bed*

"Well," Mr. Sheldon says. "Well." Mr. Sheldon is making a face that Dr. Tanglewood has not explained to me yet in face reading class.

"*Well*," Rose repeats, "*Well*."

"My goodness. Okay. Michael. What you heard was a song. A song is a short piece of music with words, that are meant to be sung. Michael, did you like the song that you heard?"

"I didn't understand it," Michael whispers.

"Thank goodness for that," Mr Sheldon says. "Let's move on to you, Isaac. What was your musical link?"

I look directly into Mr. Sheldon's eyes. He tells me good job for making eye contact, so I thank him very much then tell him, "Good job for you too, Mr. Sheldon."

"Go on Isaac, what did you learn?" he asks me again.

"I learned how to play music," I say.

"You did? Your website had instructions for playing music?"

"No. There were no instructions."

"No instructions? Then how did you learn to play music from the website?"

"I heard the music. Now, I know how to play the music."

Mr. Sheldon shakes his head. "I think it may be more complicated than that, Isaac. People take lessons for many years to learn how to play an instrument."

"Okay," I tell him. I look down at my watch. "Recess is in twenty minutes."

"In twenty minutes, yes, thank you Isaac, but first we have a special treat. Today, we're all going to have an opportunity to make music! Please follow me across the hall to the music room where Mrs. Jensen is waiting.

Mrs. Jensen is our music teacher. She is very fat but no one is allowed to say that.

When we get across the hall I see the following: one piano-Yamaha brand, one guitar-Fender brand, one drum set-no brand name showing-consisting of six drums varying in size and shape, and one box of small shiny metal instruments, marked, *Percussion.*

"Everyone, please pick your instrument," Mrs. Jensen says.

No one picks an instrument. Mr. Sheldon walks Michael over to the guitar and helps him put the strap around his neck. Mrs. Jensen leads Rose to the drums. I sit down on the bench in front of the piano. I close my eyes so that I can remember the song from my link. I put my fingers on the keys and press down. I do this five times before I find the right spot to begin.

I hear Mr. Sheldon telling Michael that the guitar is played by strumming the strings. Mrs. Jensen is explaining to Rose that the drums are percussion instruments, just like the triangles and tambourines in the box. "Hold the drum sticks like this, Rose," she says.

I move my fingers across the keys. Sounds are coming out from the back of the instrument. I am careful to keep my eyes closed so that I can remember the numbers in my head. The numbers come in different groupings; one two three-one two three, four, five, six seven eight-one two three-one two three-one two three, four five and six, seven eight, one two three...

If you were to open the top of the piano, you would see the following things:

Strings: Every sound the piano makes comes from a vibrating string. The keys of the keyboard are connected to the strings. Push down a key, get a sound.

Hammers: Press a key, a hammer flies up, hitting the vibrating string.

Soundboard: This is a thin, wide piece of wood. The soundboard amplifies the sound of the string so that it can be heard.

Dampers: Stops the vibration of the string when the finger is lifted from a pressed key.

All of theses things are happening as I play the piano. I like knowing about them. I like playing the song I heard on my link. I like playing the piano.

I finish the song and open my eyes. Michael is removing the strings from the guitar and chewing on the neck strap. Rose is walking the perimeter of the room, tapping each electrical outlet with a drumstick as she passes by. Mrs. Jensen and Mr. Sheldon are standing behind me. "Are you sure?" she asks him. "I'm one hundred percent positive. He doesn't take lessons," Mr. Sheldon answers back. "Issac, where did you learn that song? Did you learn it from your link?"

I tell Mr. Sheldon that I did learn it from my link and that the song is called, "Rondo Alla Turca," and was written by Wolfgang Amadeus Mozart, an Austrian composer born in the year 1756, deceased in the year 1791.

Mr. Sheldon asks me if I can play the song again. I check my watch. Ten minutes until recess. I tell him that the song takes four minutes and three seconds to play, so there is time. I close my eyes and put my fingers on the keyboard, only this time, I don't have to search for the correct starting place.

When I finish playing the song and open my eyes, Mrs. Jensen is crying. Mr. Sheldon is on the phone with Mother.

"Mrs. Newton, you better get down here, right away. No, no, it's just- I can't explain it. But hurry, please."

Mrs. Jensen is making her sad face, but Mr. Sheldon is making his happy face. I cannot tell if something good or something bad is happening. My stomach hurts, like when I look at the rainbow ball.

Michael sits down beside me on the bench, and whispers in my ear.

"eTunes is your number one music source. We have everything, from Hip-Hop to classic, R&B to metal. Grammy award winners, pop stars, country crooners, opera divas; get it all on eTunes. Click here for a free demonstration." He whispers his link so quietly, I can barely hear his voice over Mrs. Jensen's crying.

I went to recess with Rose and Michael, but after that, Mr. Sheldon brought me back to the music room. Since 2:37 in the afternoon, I have been listening to songs on the computer, then playing them on the piano. So far, I have played the following songs:

"Ode to Joy," by Ludwig Van Beethoven

"Moonlight Sonata," also by Ludwig Van Beethoven

"Passacaglia," by George Frideric Handel

"Sonata Number Sixteen in C Major," by W. A. Mozart

"Claire De Lune," by Claude Debussy

"Nocturne in E Flat Major," by Frederic Chopin

and

"I Guess That's Why They Call it the Blues," by Sir Elton John

I am taking a break from playing when Mother runs through the door of the music room.

"What is it? What's happening? Isaac, are you okay?" The heel on her left boot is broken and her scarf is trailing out behind her; the end where the yarn splits into sections is dragging the floor. "What's happening? Somebody speak!"

"Hi, Mother," I say. I am reading my favorite book, *How the Dung Beetle uses the Milky Way to Navigate the Universe.* "I can play the piano now," I tell her."

"What, Isaac? What? What's going on?" Mr. Sheldon and Mrs. Jensen take Mother by the arm and lead her to the corner. From their conversation, I hear the following words: link, surprise, possible savant, splinter skills, Mozart, piano, and *fuck*.

Mother comes over to me and bends down. "Isaac, is it true? Can you play the piano?"

"Yes, Mother. I just started playing. I like playing."

"Can you play something for me?"

"Not actually. I am taking a break now. I am reading about the Dung beetle. See?" I try to show Mother my book but she pushes it away.

"Please, Isaac? It's important to me. Look, I'm making my begging face, like a puppy dog."

Mother's puppy dog face makes me laugh because it is *so* funny. "Please?" she says again, sticking out her bottom lip and placing her hands to the side of her head for dog ears.

"Okay," I tell her, laughing, "but just one more song. I am *very* tired."

"Thank you, Isaac, thank you so much." Mother walks me to the piano, then sits down on the bench beside me.

"What should I play?" I ask.

"Why don't you try this one, Isaac. It's called, "Liebestraum Number Three in A-flat Major, Dream of Love," Mr. Sheldon tells me. He leans his ipod against the music desk of the piano. I close my eyes to listen. Music fills the room. Music. Is. Everywhere.

When the song is finished playing on Mr. Sheldon's ipod, I move my fingers along the keys to find the starting place. When I find it, I close my eyes and begin to play. The Liebe-straum is played all over the keyboard; my hands must move from top to bottom. When I reach over Mother to get to the lower keys, she moves back, leaning away from the piano to make room.

After I finish playing the Liebestraum, I look down at my watch; five o'clock. "Time to go." I tell this to Mother, Mr. Sheldon and Mrs. Jensen. I pull the lid down over the keys of the piano, hiding them underneath. "Time to go," I say again, but no one moves. "Mother, time to go." Still, no response. So, I yell, "TIME TO GO, M-O-T-H-E-R!"

Mother jumps up from the bench. "Okay Isaac, okay." She grabs my Dung Beetle book from the floor. *Holy shit*, she says, then *mother fucker*. After that, we are out the door.

Mother is on the phone, so I eat my dinner alone at the table; grilled cheese with tater-tots. First, she talks to Mr. Sheldon. Second, she talks to Mrs. Jensen. Third, she talks to Father. Fourth, she talks to Doctor Tanglewood. Fifth, she talks to her mother in Florida; Grandmother Pat. Grandmother Pat is a loud talker. I can hear her voice coming through the ear piece of the phone. "Well, holy, moley!" she says to Mother. "Do you think he'll get to be on the *Today Show*?"

While mother is talking to Grandmother Pat, I test all the outlets in our apartment. "Still working!" I shout, each time my circuit tester lights up.

The next day is school again, but this time, I am on a different schedule. Instead of occupational therapy with Mrs. Cardamom, I am taken directly to the music room. Mrs. Jensen is there talking with a man. "Ah, here he is!" Mrs. Jensen tells the man when I walk into the room.

The man tells me that his name is Mr. Itsak Carrol and that he is an instructor of piano at The Julliard School. "Do you like Dung beetles?" I ask him.

"Dung beetles?" he asks me back.

"Yes. I am reading a book about Dung beetles. I like them very much."

"What do you like about the Dung beetle, Isaac?" Mr. Itsak Carrol asks me.

I think about Mr. Itsak Carrol's question. While I am thinking it over, I ask *him* another question.

"Do you have a circuit tester?"

"A circuit tester? Why no. Do you have a circuit tester, Isaac?"

"Yes. I do. Where is Mrs. Cardamom? Why am I not having occupational therapy with Mrs. Cardamom? I should be having occupational therapy with Mrs. Cardamom now."

Mr. Itsak Carrol is wearing brown shoes. The shoes have tassels instead of laces and slots for pennies. The penny in the right shoe is less visible than the penny in the left shoe. Abraham Lincoln is the president whose face is on the penny. Abraham Lincoln was the sixteenth president of The United States. The penny is an American currency worth one cent.

"Isaac, I have been told that you are a very special young man. I understand that yesterday you sat down to the piano and began to play musical compositions that take most people many years of study and practice to master. Have you heard of The Julliard School?"

I shake my head left to right for, *no.*

"At The Julliard School, I work with special children, children who are supremely, musically talented. Mrs. Jensen asked me here today to listen to you play, to see if you are perhaps a candidate to study at my school. What do you think about that?"

I shrug my shoulders. "I need to have occupational therapy with Mrs. Cardamom first, please. Everyday, I start with Mrs. Cardamom, first," I tell Mr. Itsak Carrol. The hem of his pants on his left leg is coming undone, just to the side of his inner ankle.

"Could you play the piano for me first, before you have your therapy?"

"No thank you."

"Are you sure, Isaac? This could be very important."

"NO THANK YOU, MR. ITSAK CARROL! I, NEED, TO, HAVE, OCCUPATIONAL, THERAPY, WITH, MRS. CARDAMOM! FIRST! PLEASE!"

Mrs. Jensen takes me to Mrs. Cardamom. "Isaac!" she says. "I didn't think I was going to get to see you today. I'm so glad you're here!"

I tell her that she will *always* see me first, Monday through Friday, then I run to the bin and pick the blue ball.

"Catch hands up, Isaac!" Mrs. Cardamom yells.

"Catch hands up, Mrs. Cardamom!" I yell back.

I almost catch the ball thirteen times. Mrs. Cardamom smiles at me with her big teeth.

"Nice job, Isaac!" she tells me.

"Nice job, Mrs. Cardamom!" I tell her back.

After lunch it is back to the music room. Mother and Father have come to hear me play. Like Mr. Sheldon, Mr. Itsak Carrol has an ipod. He hooks it up to two speakers and presses *play*. "Please listen carefully, Isaac," Mr. Itsak Carrol tells me, as the music begins to play.

When the song is over, I move my fingers along the keys, then begin. Strings, hammers, soundboard, dampers. Strings, hammers, soundboard, dampers.

This is the way the day goes; strings, hammers, soundboard, dampers.

At five o'clock, when Mother and Father take me to see Doctor Tanglewood, Mr. Itsak Carrol is already there. I wait outside in reception with Cathy while Mother and Father go into Dr. Tanglewood's office to talk.

"Got your nose, Isaac!" Cathy says, pretending to get my nose. *Got your nose* is a joke, a game. "Got your nose, Cathy!" I joke back, reaching for her nose. Like with many of the games Cathy and I play, there is no way to determine a winner.

After twenty-two minutes and eleven seconds, Mr. Itsak Carrol comes out of Doctor Tanglewood's office. "Good-bye Isaac," he says to me. "I will see you again very soon, I hope." He has lost the penny from his right shoe; the loose thread of his pants has given way.

"Come on in, Isaac," Dr. Tanglewood tells me through the open door.

Mother and Father are waiting for me on the couch. "Here Isaac, sit here," Father says scooting over from Mother and patting the now empty place between them. The leather of the couch is warm and when I am settled into the cushions, I realize how sleepy I am. Dr. Tanglewood starts.

"Isaac, do you know why your school schedule has been altered the last two days?"

"No."

"Your school schedule has been altered because you have a remarkable talent. Your remarkable talent is your ability to play music on the piano."

"Okay."

"This is a very rare talent, Isaac. Do you know what I mean by rare?"

I shake my head.

"It means that very few people in the world have the ability to play the piano the way that you do."

"How many?" I want to know.

"I don't know, Isaac, but not very many."

"Could we please find out how many? I would like to know." Dr. Tanglewood looks at Mother and Father. Father tells me that sure, we'll find out how many, we'll check on that for sure, then he calls me "sport" and messes my hair. I smooth it back down the way that I like it, which is the way it was before he messed it.

On the way home I find a twenty dollar bill on the curb. "I wish I'd find twenty bucks," Mother tells me.

The trick is to always look down. That way, you can see the money and you do not have to worry so much about the faces.

Father comes to our apartment for dinner. When I answer the door I ask him, "Did you call twenty-four hours in advance?" Before Father can answer, Mother yells at me from the kitchen, "It's okay, Isaac. You can let him in."

Mother has made spaghetti for dinner. Father opens a bottle of wine and lets me have a sip. "Yucky!" I tell him, as I make my sour face.

Mother and Father talk to me about my remarkable and rare talent. They tell me I am what is called a musical savant. They tell me that I have a splinter skill and that my particular splinter skill is music. A splinter skill is a talent that is unrelated to the rest of my life. Father says that the word *savant* is French for *savior* and that he looked it up in a dictionary knowing that I would want to know the meaning.

When they are finished telling me about my remarkable and rare talent, I ask if we have anything for dessert and if we do, could it be ice cream. Mother tells me that we do not have any ice cream but that we have do have fruit salad with poppy seed dressing. I tell Mother that I hope there are strawberries in the fruit salad and she says that there are. The average strawberry contains two hundred seeds.

At bedtime, Mother *and* Father tuck me in.

"Isaac, starting tomorrow, you'll be going to see Mr. Itsak Carrol at The Julliard School. He will work with you on the piano," Father tells me.

"Work with me?"

"He will be your teacher."

"But I do not need a teacher. I already know how to play."

"Right, right," Father says, sitting down on the bed beside me. "You do already know how to play, but, Mr. Carrol will teach you things that you don't know how to do, like read and compose music."

I don't know what those words mean. Read music? But music is something that you hear. What does compose mean? I think I feel my stomach starting to hurt. I do not want to go. "No thank you, Father." I tell him. "No thank you."

"Isaac..." Mother says.

"First in the morning, I have occupational therapy with Mrs. Cardamom."

"You'll still see Mrs. Cardamom...."

"Second, I have lunch."

"You'll still have lunch."

"Third, learning. Fourth recess. Fifth, learning. Sixth, Doctor Tanglewood."

"You'll still do all of those things Isaac, just not everyday. Three days a week your schedule will be different. You'll go to Julliard to work with Mr. Carrol. The other two days of the week will be the same. No different at all."

"No thank you, Mother. No thank you, Father."

Mother is making her angry face. Father's face has not changed. They both stare at me. Suddenly, I remember what I wanted to tell them earlier about the Dung beetle.

"Is now a good time to tell you people how the Dung beetle uses The Milky Way to navigate the Universe?" I ask.

"For fuck's sake," Mother says. Father says that no, it really is not.

"Go to bed, Isaac. Sleep tight. We'll talk more in the morning," Mother tells me.

"Okay, but *sleeping tight* is not something I can really do," I tell them as they go. "I do not even know what sleeping tight means."

"Just go to bed, Isaac," Mother says, then shuts the door.

Through the closed door of my bedroom I can hear Mother and Father arguing.

Mother says: You've never worried enough about him. You've never worried the right way.

Father says: That's not fair, Laura. I worry about him plenty, but in my own way.

Mother says: He doesn't even want to do it. Why should we make him do it?

Father says: This is a shot, a real shot for Isaac. A way for him to be independent some day.

Mother says: No way. I won't let him end up on *The Today Show* or as some download on You Tube entitled, *Idiot Savant plays Chopin with eyes closed* or *Human player piano*. Not my baby. Not my Isaac.

Father says: No one is that cruel, Laura. No one would do that.

Mother says: You're so fucking naïve, Rob. Everyone's that cruel. Everyone would do that.

Father says: We're just going in circles here, complete circles.

"Just like the Dung beetle!" I shout from my bedroom. "When he is blind-folded and forced to navigate the universe in total darkness!"

"Go to bed, Isaac!" Mother *and* Father shout.

The front door slams. "Finally!" mother yells. "You're the right kind of mad!"

But Father does not answer back; he is already gone.

In the morning, Mother is standing in the doorway of my bedroom holding my suitcase. " Surprise kiddo! We're going on a trip, just you and me," she says.

"Today is Thursday," I tell her. "I have occupational therapy first on Thursdays."

"Yep, and you have lunch second and learning third and recess fourth and learning fifth and Doctor Tanglewood sixth-I know all that. But today, we're going on a trip so those things will have to wait until later. Come on, get a move on."

"When later?" I ask her.

"Later, later," she tells me, but *later, later* is not a real measurement of time, so I do not know what she means.

The airport is loud and people are hurrying all about, knocking into my shoulders and touching my backpack with their bodies. "I do not like any of this," I tell the woman taking mine and Mother's tickets. "Enjoy your flight, cutie pie," the woman tells me. "Next!"

Our plane is a *Boeing 737*. There are twenty-three rows of seats, six seats per row-one hundred thirty-eight seats in all. Mother and I sit on the left side of the plane, row fourteen, almost exactly in the middle. She lets me have the seat closest to the window. The wing of the airplane stretches out below. On the ground, men are loading suitcases and boxes into the bottom of the airplane.

"Where are we going, Mother?" I ask her.

"To the land of the alligators, kiddo. Florida."

"Alligators live in the Southeastern region of the United States. This includes Florida, Louisiana, the southern tip of Arkansas..."

"Oh, my, God," Mother says, putting her earphones over

her ears.

When we get to the airport in Florida, Grandmother Pat is waiting for us.

"Shake it on over here, baby boy!" she tells me. "Give your grandmother a hug."

I look up at Mother. "Do it," she says.

Grandmother Pat smells like suntan lotion and sandwich bread. Her hair is yellow and her lips are bright pink. She is suffocating me. "I am suffocating!" I tell them. Mother says, "No, you're not."

Grandmother Pat says, "Whew wee, you sure have grown!"

Outside in the parking lot, Grandmother Pat leads us to a car without a top. Mother tells me that a car without a top is called a convertible. "Riding in a convertible is the only way to travel when you're in Florida," she tells me. "There's nothing like feeling the wind in your hair."

I hesitate. I have never been in a topless car before.

"Relax," Grandmother Pat tells me. "Climb in, your head won't fall off."

The wind blows Mother's hair all around her head. She puts sunglasses on her face that cover her eyes. When she raises her arms above her head, Grandmother Pats laughs. "That's my baby girl," she tells Mother. "It sure is good to have you home!"

On the way to Grandmother Pat's house we pass a sign; *Welcome to Polk County, Florida's largest producer of Citrus.* On the sign is a picture of an orange with a human face, arms and legs. With one hand the orange man waves at passer byers, with the other, he holds a glass of juice. "Wave to the orange man, Laura honey!" Grandmother Pat tells Mother.

"Hello, orange man!" Mother yells, as we go speeding by.

Rows and rows of fruit trees line the road. The car is moving so quickly that the trees become a blur; the orange of the fruit and the green of the leaves mixing with the blue of the sky. Like Mrs. Cardamom's rainbow ball.

"Grandmother Pat, could you slow down?" I yell. I have to yell because driving in a convertible car is a loud situation. She looks over at Mother, who shrugs. "He wants to count the rows," Mother tells her.

"Oh," Grandmother Pat laughs, then speeds up. "Not down here, kiddo. In Florida, you don't count."

Grandmother Pat's house is surrounded by an orange farm, the same farm where Mother used to steal oranges.

"When it was dark, I would crawl under a hole in the fence and shimmy over to the trees on my belly. I would lay there in the shadows, until I was sure no one was watching, then I'd find a tree with a ladder that some picker forgot to put up and climb right up to the top, grabbing all the fruit I wanted. Come on Isaac, let's go see if that hole is still there."

I follow mother to the back of Grandmother Pat's yard. On the way to see if that hole is still there I see palm trees, bougainvillea vines and scruffy palmetto plants, but no alligators. "Look, Isaac," Mother tells me. "The hole's still there!"

The hole is small and Mother is big. How did you fit through the hole?" I ask her.

"I was a lot smaller then, about your size. Want to see if you can fit through the hole?"

"No thank you."

"Oh, come on. Where's your sense of adventure?"

"No thank you, Mother. No thank you."

Mother crosses her arms over her chest. "You're no fun, mister party pooper," she tells me.

After dinner Mother and Grandmother Pat float on rafts in the swimming pool. Mother's raft is green; Grandmother Pat's is pink.

"Come on in, the water's fine, sugar," Grandmother Pat tells me. Mother and Grandmother Pat drink from tall glasses with miniature, purple umbrellas sticking out from the top. "Come on, Isaac. You're a good swimmer," Mother says.

"Are there any alligators in the swimming pool?" I ask Mother. She tells me that no, there certainly are not.

"I was hoping to see an alligator," I tell her.

Mother paddles her hand through the water, slowly turning her raft in a circle.

"No thank you, Isaac. No thank you," she tells me, then takes a long swig from her drink.

That night I dream about a Dung beetle, who on a cloudy night, gets lost in the universe. I wake up screaming and when I tell mother what is wrong she tells me that it was all just a dream baby, just a bad dream. But I am still scared and upset.

"Do you understand?" I ask her. "The Dung beetle has to

have the light of The Milky Way in order to navigate the universe or else he gets lost and keeps circling back to the dung pile."

"So?"

"The Dung beetle wants to navigate in a straight line *away* from the dung pile. The dung pile is dangerous. There are other Dung beetles there, competing for the dung. The Dung beetles fight, they go in circles. If the Dung beetle can not see The Milky Way, he can not get out of the dung. THE DUNG BEETLE IS TRAPPED!"

"Okay, okay, Isaac," Mother tells me, pulling me close and suffocating me. "Okay, okay."

"He has to have the light!"

"I get it. Darkness sucks. Bad things happen in the dark. I get it, now calm down."

Mother rocks me back and forth in the darkness. After a while I feel wet, stuck to her skin.

"Florida is too hot," I tell her. "I think I am melting."

"No you're not, Isaac," Mother tells, me kissing my head. "You're not melting."

"A straight line out of the dung pile. That is what the Dung beetle wants."

"He's not the only one," Mother says, letting me go.

In the morning, Mother is busy on the phone. First, she calls my school. Second, she calls Mr. Itsak Carrol. Third, she calls Father. "Autism is a dung pile," she tells Father over the phone.

While Mother talks to Father on the phone for a one hour,

fifteen minutes and twenty-nine seconds, Grandmother Pat
sits with me at the table buttering toast and smearing it with
marmalade jam.

"Try this," she tells me, handing over the bread. "I think
that if you could eat the sun, it would taste like marmalade."

"You cannot eat the sun. The core temperature of the sun is
five-thousand, five-hundred, and five degrees Celsius."

"You don't say?" Grandmother Pat says. "But what do you
think about the marmalade?"

"Mmmm, good," I tell her. "Sweet."

When Mother is finished talking to Father she tells Grandmother Pat that she needs some time to think. "You got it,
sweet stuff," Grandmother Pat tells her. "You stay here and
Isaac and I will entertain ourselves elsewhere. How about we
go find some alligators to look at, Isaac?"

"Alligators, Grandmother Pat?"

"Yes sir. I know just the place."

"It's safe, right?" Mother asks.

Grandmother Pat waves her hand in the air. "It's a petting
zoo, Laura. How dangerous can it be?"

The petting zoo is 16.9 miles away from Grandmother Pat's
house. We start with the zebras.

"Here Isaac, feed him this," Grandmother Pat tells me,
handing over a carrot.

With a snap!, the zebra takes the carrot. The zebra has enormous teeth, just like Mrs. Cardamom.

"I think this zebra is beautiful," I tell Grandmother Pat. "It looks like my teacher."

Grandmother Pat laughs. "Well, she must be one heck of a beautiful lady!"

Second, we see the Peacocks and Guinea hens. I don't like the way the Guinea hens peck at my feet; Grandmother Pat has to carry me out of the pen.

"Quit screaming directly in my ear, Isaac. I'm getting us out of here as fast as I can," she tells me, trying to squeeze both of us out through the gate at the same time. "Suck in, Isaac, we're too fat," she says when we don't fit through.

Third, we visit the big cats. They lay spread out in their cages, stretching and mewing.

"Well, those aren't nothing but ordinary, overgrown house cats," Grandmother Pat tells me. "This place is a rip off!"

Fourth is goats. The black goat will not stop chewing on my shirt. "What did I tell you about that screaming, Isaac?" Grandmother Pat asks as she carries me out, her free hand covering her left ear. "I sure wish I'd known I was going to need my earplugs."

We come to a sign that reads, *Alligators-Beware!* "That a-way," Grandmother Pat says, pointing to a trail leading downward through the tall grass.

At the end of the path is a man standing on a wooden platform built out over a pond. "You come to feed the gators?" the man asks.

"Why, yes we have," Grandmother Pat tells the man. "I've got a real alligator expert here and he is ready!"

The man bends down to look at me. "You know about the egg tooth, young man?"

The man is old and his face has thick, floppy bends that fold over. "Yes," I tell the man. "I know about the egg tooth."

"Good. I want everyone to know about the egg tooth. Just imagine, being born with exactly the right tool for the job. Now then, here's your meat."

The man puts a long stick in my hand. On the end of the stick is a piece of raw meat. Sitting on the piece of raw meat is a fly. I move the stick in closer to get a better look at the compound eye of the fly, but the movement scares it away.

The man leads us to the end of the platform. I lean over to look past the edge and there they are-real Florida alligators!

"Would you look at all of those gators," Grandmother Pat says. "Just look at those snappers!"

The alligators lay in a pile. The alligator on top of the pile blinks his eyes. The man motions me forward.

"Now, you, young man, come on over here and hold that stick *waaaay* out. No, further out than that. Good. That's far enough and we'll just see...."

All of the sudden, a swarm of alligators jumps up out of the water!

"...what happens."

My stick bounces off the pile of alligator bodies, then sinks down slowly into the muddy water.

"That sure was fast!" Grandmother Pat laughs. Her voice sounds extra breathy and she is holding her right hand over her heart.

"Always is," the man tells her. "Got to keep your hands out the way. *Out the way!*"

The man walks with Grandmother Pat and me to The

Petting Zoo Cafe. On the way there he tells us about his son.

"Yea, he was always real good with his hands, could take apart anything and then put it back together. Never had many friends, always felt more at home with his books. After Florida State he joined the navy and now he's designing war ships. Lives in Virginia Beach with a half-wild, stray cat he calls Samson. I say, 'Son, why don't you get you a cat you can touch? Plenty a cat out there needin' a good home.' But he says that the cat he's got is just fine, that they understand each other well enough."

"It takes all kinds," Grandmother Pat says.

"Don't it though?" the man says back.

At The Petting Zoo Café, Grandmother Pat buys me a hot dog and a cola.

"Want some ketchup or something on that, Isaac?"

"No thank you, Grandmother Pat."

"What about some mustard?"

"No thank you."

"Relish? That dog's gonna be awful dry without something on it."

"No."

"Here Isaac, let me have it. I'll doctor it up for you. You'll like it."

"NO THANK YOU GRANDMOTHER PAT! I, DO, NOT, WANT, ANYTHING, ON, MY, HOT, DOG!"

Grandmother Pat tells me I can sit over there on that piano bench and have some time to myself, then she steps outside to call Mother. I can hear her part of the conversation through the screen door of the café.

"Well," she says, "he just freaked out over pickle relish, but other than that, everything's good." Then, after a pause, "No, he did not get eaten by an alligator."

The old man comes out from behind the counter and sits down on the bench beside me. "Can you play?" he asks me.

"Yes," I tell him.

"Would you then? It's been so long since this old piano's been a-played. My sweet, departed wife was the pianist and I sure miss her playing."

I put my hot dog down beside me. "Okay. What should I play?"

"Well, that depends, what do you know?"

I think for a minute. "I know Mozart."

"Mozart? Well, that sounds good."

I play Mozart in the order that Mr. Itsak Carrol's ipod played Mozart. First: "Sonata Number sixteen in C Major." Second: "Rondo Alla Turca." Third: "Piano Sonata Number eleven in A Major."

When I am finished I reach for my hot dog. "That is all the Mozart I know," I tell the man.

"Young man, how old are you?" he asks me.

"I am seven years, two months and twenty-one days old," I tell him. My hot dog has become cold, but I take a bite from it anyway.

"Well, you certainly have the right tools for the job," he tells me, standing up and wiping the corners of his eyes with a paper napkin. "That was good; real special. I thank you for playing for me, young fellow."

"You are welcome." I tell the man. He makes both a sad and a happy face and I wonder which is he; sad or happy? Faces can be complicated sometimes.

Grandmother Pat comes back into the cafe. She is rubbing a tube of lipstick across her lips.

"Time to go, Isaac," she says, pressing her lips together. The color is the same bright pink she had on at the airport and matches her fingernails, her shirt, her shoes, her handbag and her sun-visor.

"Nice to meet you both!" The old man yells after us as we leave The Petting Zoo Café.

When we get back to Grandmother's Pat's house, there is a man there with Mother. He is older than Mother, but not as old as the old man from the petting zoo. His skin is very tan and his feet are bare. He and Mother are sitting at the table by the pool drinking orange colored drinks and laughing very loudly.

"Well, who is this?" Grandmother Pat asks mother.

"Mother, this is your neighbor, Mr. Donovan. He owns the orange farm next door."

"Please," Mr. Donovan says, taking off his hat. "Call me Jessie."

"Oh, Jessie!" Grandmother Pat says. "This is so embarrassing, living here all these years and never having met you. I've meant to go over and introduce myself a thousand times!"

"Now, don't you feel badly about that at all, it's me who should be embarrassed. Good Lord, a house full of beautiful ladies and here I am just now knowing about it." Mr. Jessie Donovan holds out his hand to shake Grandmother Pat's. When the hand shake is finished, Mr. Jessie Donovan holds on. Grandmother tells him she sure is glad to finally meet him and asks if something special has brought him over. He looks at Mother and says, *in a way*, then begins to tell the story.

Mr. Jessie Donovan said he was making his final walk of the day around the grove checking on the Valencia when he heard something crying. At first, he thought it was a severely injured animal and regretted not having his gun on him to put the poor creature out of its misery. He walked toward the crying sound, fearing what he would find and that was when he saw it; a grown woman's butt and pair of legs sticking out from that hole in the fence, that very same hole he'd been intending to mend for ages!

"Miss, you okay?" Mr. Jessie Donovan asked the butt and pair of legs.

"What the fuck do you think?" the butt and pair of legs answered back. (When Mr. Jessie Donovan told this part, Grandmother Pat made a gasping sound, then started to laugh. "Your mouth," she said to Mother, then laughed some more.)

Now, back to the story.

Mr. Jessie Donovan examined the situation carefully-carefully enough to realize that the person attached to the butt and pair of legs could have easily made it back through the hole if that person's pockets weren't bulging so with stolen oranges.

"If you'll just allow me to take the oranges out of your pockets, I think we can slide you through the hole," Mr. Jessie Donovan told the butt and pair of legs. But the butt and pair of legs said back, "No fucking way. These oranges are mine!" That was when Mr. Jessie Donovan realized that the butt and pair of legs meant business and the best any of them could hope for was for him to push the butt and pair of legs toward Grandmother Pat's house, a lovely lady whose name he did not know until now, and hope for the best where the oranges were concerned.

Well, sure as day, when he was pushing the butt and pair of legs through to the other side of the fence, the oranges started popping and squirting juice everywhere; concurrently, the butt and pair of legs started spurting out profanity so proficiently vile, that Mr. Jessie Donovan, a former Merchant Marine, found himself more than a little impressed, but not so much so that he would ever be comfortable repeating such language to a lady as fine and distinguished as my grandmother Pat, of course.

Finally, after all that cursing and wiggling, the butt and pair of legs made it through to the other side. While Mr. Jessie Donovan, who by this point was worn out as thunder, was leaning up against the fence trying to catch his breath, the butt and pair of legs produced a complete upper body making a full person and guess who it turned out to be? Mother!

Mother poked her head back through the hole and told Mr. Jessie Donovan that either he could have her arrested or he could come over and keep her company drinking *Mai Tai's* until her mother and son got home from the petting zoo and that is what Mr. Jessie Donovan has been doing ever since. And, he brought mother a bushel of his finest Valencia, so that she would not have to steal his oranges any more.

A bushel is a United States customary measurement and is equal to 35.24 liters.

At the end of the story, Grandmother Pat's face glows red and she fans herself with a magazine she picked up from the table. "Won't you stay for dinner?" she asks Mr. Jessie Donovan, her yellow hair spreading out in every direction with each wave.

During dinner, Grandmother Pat and Mr. Jessie Donovan make their happy faces at each other; *a lot*. Mother says, "Come here Isaac, sit on my lap."

When I do she squeezes me very hard around the middle. "You are suffocating me!" I tell her.

"I know, Isaac," Mother says, kissing me on the back of my head.

After dinner, Mother asks me to look at the stars with her. We drag Grandmother Pat's lounge chairs to the front yard and look up at the sky.

"You can actually see the stars here, unlike in Brooklyn where there's too much interference," Mother tells me.

The sound of Grandmother Pat's and Mr. Jessie Donovan's laughter travels from the backyard to the front. After a while their laughter turns into talking, then their talking into whispers, then their whispers into silence. Eventually, all that I can I can hear is a faint sound of splashing coming from the pool.

"Grandmother Pat and Mr. Donovan are swimming in the pool," Mother tells me. "So, we better stay out with the stars."

I decide to be very still and quiet and listen to the sounds that are happening in Grandmother Pat's yard. I hear crickets and frogs chirping, and something moving in the bougainvillea growing up the side of the house-probably a snake or a lizard. I think to myself that these sounds are a kind of music, and it makes me feel happy to know that Mother and

I are surrounded by music, which is something that I enjoy now-like testing outlets with my circuit tester- and that music is here for us to listen to any time that we want.

After a few minutes Mother asks, "Isaac, when you close your eyes to play the piano, what do you see, in your brain I mean?"

"In my brain?"

"Yea, when you close your eyes. I know you told Mr. Carroll that you hear numbers, but does your brain show you pictures or colors or anything like that?"

"No."

"Nothing at all? Really?"

"No."

"How wonderful," she tells me, closing her own eyes.

I tilt my head back to look into the night. The Milky Way spreads out before us, shining, twinkling. "There is no way to count the stars," I say. Mother nods her head. "I know."

When Mother puts me to bed, she asks me to tell her everything I know about the Dung beetle and how it uses The Milky Way to navigate the universe.

"Look directly into my eyes when you tell me, Isaac. Please, don't look away, not even for a second."

"I will mother," I tell her. Mother is making her happy face, so I make sure that I do.

Mother wakes me at 6:30 am. She has packed my suitcase and has it sitting by the door.

"We're going home now, Isaac. Time to face the music, so to speak. Are you ready?" she asks me.

I stretch my arms over my head, then tell her that I am.

"I am glad that I got to see an alligator," I say, getting out of bed.

"Me too," Mother smiles down at me, handing me my shirt.

Grandmother Pat drives us to the airport in her convertible car. As we pass the orange man sign, Mother stands up and yells, *goodbye, orange man,* before Grandmother Pat even has a chance to remind her.

Mother and Father have decided not to get a divorce. We have moved into a larger apartment here in Brooklyn and bought a piano; Yamaha brand. I practice playing the piano three hours a day. Mozart is my favorite composer. My circuit tester was lost in the move, but I keep looking for it.

Grandmother Pat married Mr. Jessie Donovan. Each Friday, Mother receives a box of Florida oranges in the mail. On the outside of the box, Mr Jessie Donovan writes; *to the finest butt and pair of legs in Brooklyn.*

Now, when Mother see the oranges at the farmer's market on Atlantic Avenue, she makes her happy face and walks straight on by.

"Just like the Dung beetle," she tells me.

"Just like the Dung beetle," I tell her back.

The Business of Cutting

The tattoos began as a way for her to hide the cutting. Each night after she had finished, she would get into her father's car and drive down to the south side of town where the parlors stayed open until the sun began its predictable ascension into place as the center of the known universe.

She was no one important, she knew this. Not a fire fighter never forgetting Nine Eleven or a soldier missing his girl, a floral sounding name like Rose or Heather, ground into the flesh of his arm as if the creation of the tattoo would somehow be enough to keep them united over miles and across time-zones.

She wasn't romantic or naive. She didn't believe another tattoo would change her persona or alter the course of her life, or even that its place on her skin would keep her from cutting again. But as she walked the floor of the parlor studying the flash hanging on the walls, she reveled in the normalcy of it all, that she, like the other customers in the shop, was just a regular person making a mundane, if not extraneous choice. A decision that didn't matter so much, but one that she could hold to, even if the rest of her moments seemed to have gotten away.

There was no special method or preference she employed when adopting a design. In fact, often she would choose a configuration that made absolutely no sense to her, going so far as to picking a composition she didn't even like, such as the Fleur de lis she wore wrapped like a brace around her ankle; she had no particular affinity for France. Or the time she choose a rabbit, caught perfectly in the moment of popping from the hat, the never ceasing expression of surprise on the bunny's face disturbing; the stiff erection of its ears nearly bringing her to tears each time she backed up to the mirror to study its place upon her shoulder.

It was in the confusion of these decisions that she felt truly the happiest, a reaction she couldn't explain anymore than she could account for the rabbit. Nothing about it made sense, yet somehow it did; the joy she felt preparing her for the inevitable moment when the needle would meet the placid surface of her epidermis, and the Parietal Lobe of her brain would cry out in warning before finally surrendering, resolving itself to the pain.

She had a favorite artist at the parlor. Like the other tattooist working there he had chosen an alias, going by the moniker of *Rock-n-Roll*, his true identity shrouded in mystery like that of a super-hero. The name made her feel uncomfortable, as if he were trying too hard to fit into the mold poured out for him by the world. But still, she liked him. He was agreeable, easy, never asking any questions about the marks littering her body; the exact, *x- marks-the-spot*, where she would point when asked about the potential placement of a new tat. Often, after examining her wounds, the other artist would send her away, telling her to come back when the damage had healed, no one wanting to be responsible for making things worse. But never Rock-n-Roll.

The minute she walked through the door of the parlor she would begin her search for him, politely turning away the other artist offering their services until he came into her view. Smiling widely she would rush him, hoping the grin would disguise the tone of desperation she could hear in her own voice each and every time she asked if he would ink her. He always smiled back, always say that he would. Of course he would; anything for her.

She would lay on the table at his mercy, the waist band of her pants pulled down just below the hip or the sleeve of her shirt rolled up beyond her bicep muscle revealing the place she wanted him to paint and he, always a gentleman, would look just beyond the place of exposure, dutifully nodding his head in response to her request.

The night she carved the skin on her stomach into a shape slightly reminiscent of a finger nail moon, the parlor was so crowded with university students intent on committing acts of defiance before heading home for the break, that she had to wait in line for Rock-n-Roll, sitting outside the door of his room in a knock-off Herman Miller chair, one no longer possessing the ability to spin.

After a few minutes, two twenty-something girls emerged,

one looking exhilarated, the other moving slowly, dreamily, as if emerging from a fog.

"Hot damn, girl, you're getting covered. I like it, I like it a lot. It's hot," he gushed, as he led her past the girls and on inside.

"Thank you," she replied, an answer seeming genuinely inappropriate, but not used to receiving compliments, the best she could come up with on such short notice. She looked down at the piece of flash in her hand.

"So a snake, huh?" he asked, dipping the head of a needle into a vat of alcohol, then shaking it dry.

"It's a serpent," she corrected, pointing to the text at the bottom of the page. *Virginia's serpent*, it read, referring to another artist there at the parlor who could claim the design as that of her own.

"Where we gonna paint this one?" He was distracted, going through the bottles of pigments on the shelf, checking for greens, yellows, a blue that he would need.

She lifted her shirt to reveal the spot. When he finished his sorting he met her at the table, his eyes darting around the wound in search of usable skin.

"Yea, we can put it there," he said, a piece of long black hair falling in front of his eyes. On instinct, she looped the runaway hair behind his ear. Awkward. Neither one of them moved, her hand stuck in midair and she having absolutely no idea how to lower it back into the shelter of her lap without making even more of a scene than she already had. He recovered more quickly than she did, excusing himself momentarily, mumbling something about a particular shade he needed from another room.

By the time he came back with the blue, she had finished crying. He did her the kindest of courtesies; acting as though he didn't know.

Later at home that night she examined the design, finding that even though it was not originally his, he had signed it anyway. *R&R*, a makers mark, cut into her skin, forever marking that pound of flesh as his own.

She was dreaming of an enormous swan when the phone rang. Short of her parents weekly check in, no one called her anymore. She had seen to it herself, cultivating the isolation around her like a gardener patiently awaiting the formation of a slow growing hedge.

"Good morning!" came an annoyingly high-spirited voice from the other end. "May I speak to the person who takes care of your Internet and cable needs?"

She took the receiver from her ear and stared into it as if she could see the purveyor of this annoyance by studying the ear-piece, but when it revealed no such allusion, put the receiver back to her ear. "They don't live here anymore. I can give you their number in Florida if you want."

"Florida huh? Sounds like somebody decided they couldn't make it through another Michigan winter."

"Yea, something like that," she yawned into the phone, hoping the telemarketer would get the idea.

He didn't.

"Well, let me ask you. Are you over eighteen and able to make sound financial decisions on your own behalf?"

"No."

"To which part?"

She reviewed the string of questions in her still half-sleeping mind. "The second part," she answered.

"So, you are over eighteen?"

"Yea."

"That's a great start!"

"Terrific," she said, without really thinking that it was. There was a pause at the other end as she heard him clear his throat in anticipation of the spiel he was readying to launch into, full force.

"Let me ask you, are you happy with your Internet and cable service provider?"

She stared at the clock across the room; ten thirty. Two hours earlier than she usually woke. "I don't know. I don't have a TV or a computer so it's hard to tell."

"You don't have a TV or a computer?" he asked, his voice sounding with something, not exactly disbelief or alarm, something closer to admiration. "Well, hot dam! You must be the only person in America without a TV or a computer."

She looked at the clock again. Ten thirty-two. "I don't think you're supposed to say 'hot dam' to a potential customer."

"No, you're probably right, but I don't think a person who doesn't have a TV or a computer is a potential customer."

"This is true." Ten thirty-three. Life going by in minutes.

"Well, thank you for your time, Miss..."

"You're welcome."

"Have a nice day."

"Yea, you too."

"So, one more question. Do you think that you might buy a TV or a computer by this time tomorrow. I mean, if you do, I can call you back and check, to see if you're happy with your Internet and cable service then."

"Seriously? No. I'm not buying either."

"Why not?"

" Because I don't want to."

"Well, how do you stay informed, or keep up with friends and family?"

Ten thirty-six. He was sucking up her day. "I'm sorry, but could you please stop asking me questions? I really hate it." It occurred to her that she could hang up and she really wanted to, but for whatever, unknown reason, couldn't bring herself to do it. There was a lull from the other end of the line; she could only assume the telemarketer to be stunned into silence by her bluntness.

"Look. What's your name?" she asked, feeling the need to make amends.

"Roy."

"Okay, Roy, you sound like a really nice guy and I don't want to go all crazy on you, but you woke me up and I'm really not interested in continuing this conversation anymore. It's making my head hurt."

"Sorry."

"That's okay, I know you're just doing your job."

"Well, not really. I mean, this is my job, but it's my day job. It's not what I want to do forever. I'm a painter. I work a couple of jobs to get by, just until my art starts selling."

She leaned back into the pillow. Why was she getting into this?

"What kind of art?"

"Really, you want to know?"

"Sure Roy, what you got?"

"Well, I call it stream of consciousness art."

"I don't get it. What does it look like."

"It looks like the linear places in our brains."

She closed her eyes and tried to imagine, but it was hard-she was so newly awake. "Lines and points, but I can't picture it. What would you do with it?"

She could sense his excitement before he even spoke.

"Everything! You can do everything with it! You have these lines, figurative you know, and they meet at certain points, but they can only meet once at each point before they have to continue on and that's where I find inspiration-in the progression of the line."

"I still don't get it. It sounds like a maze. What does it look like when you paint it?"

"It looks like moments, stolen and taken away. Chance meetings, past regrets, wish you would haves, should haves, could haves, but didn't."

"Oh."

"Missed opportunities."

"Alright."

"Sore losers."

"Okay, I think I get the point." She didn't, nor did she intend to make the pun. She hoped he didn't notice and was relieved when he let it slide.

"Mainly, I paint wherever my brain takes me."

"Okay," she said in a small voice, her enthusiasm for the pursuit waining.

"Sorry," he said, reigning in his excitement. "Sometimes I get carried away. Hardly anybody ever asks about my art."

In the background she could hear the other telemarketers, their voices muffled and vague. Were they having conversations anything like this one, or were they dutifully sticking to the script? *Are you happy with your Internet and cable provider ma'am? Sir?*

"We're almost out of time. Can I call you tomorrow?" Roy asked.

"You're going to be disappointed because I am not buying a thing."

"That's fair. Talk to you then," he said, barely getting out the words before the phone went dead.

She hung the receiver back onto the phone, staring at it for several minutes as if it owed her an explanation for this latest betrayal. And though she concentrated on the theory, the phone revealed nothing of itself. She knew it wouldn't, being nothing but an empty shell waiting for bells and voices to bring it to life.

She moved over to the bay window where she sat watching the snow fall, fat white flakes coming down sideways in the wind. In just a week's time she would be flying to Florida to visit her parents over the Christmas holiday. They would fuss over her new tats, but not too much. When they told her they were giving her space they meant it, and distance, miles and miles.

The children across the street stayed out until well past dark, dancing in the snow as the wind blew it round, their little bodies spinning like spirit filled banshees before falling onto the soft, velvet carpet beneath them on the ground. *If they were my children*, she thought, *I would bring them in way before dark. Terrible things happen in the dark.*

She didn't cut herself that night, instead she sat for hours in the window looking out onto the snow, trying to imagine a design in which two intersecting lines met precisely in the middle joined together by a single point. Mother would be a line, father another, each holding tightly to the hand of the point, their child. Or was it more like progression? Getting from one stage to another by way of a single series of steps? Dr. Jekyll drinks the potion becomes Mr. Hyde? Was she getting at the essence of Roy's art, even a little?

Gingerly, with her fingertips, she traced line after line upon her arm, each time pausing when introducing a new point of progression; the waiting a temporary measure like stopping briefly for a traffic cone in the road before gradually continuing on.

Here is a man swimming, here is a shark, here the two meet, here is the blood from the bite. In another, *here is a child upon his birthday, this is the bicycle he receives as a gift, here is the fall from the bike, here is the skinned knee.*

The longer she went into the night the more elaborate the series of progressions became until she realized that the possibilities were virtually infinite.

Here is the girl walking to her car in the parking garage. Here she drops her keys. Here is the man coming from behind. Here she screams. Here he puts the knife to her throat. Here she is promising, begging. Here he is forcing her into the car.

Her finger found the scar on her shoulder, his work not hers, and the home of the perpetually surprised rabbit and his hat. *Here is the first place he used the knife.*

Next to the mark on her chest, the wound camouflaged by a heart looking more suited for a child's Valentine box than a body; a design that because of its relation to her own rendered it a cliché, one she could fully admit.

Here he won't stop though she begs him to.

She closed her eyes and through memory traced the rest of the route, finding the Gothic cross painted just above the nipple of her right breast. *On this spot she chose to commemorate the moment he put down the knife, the moment she knew what would happen next.*

Next on the path of remembrance, the Aztec sun whose disseminating rays disguise the series of scars on her wrist. *Here he is crushing her with his weight.*

Her hip; the rose tattoo, a fledgling bud only partially open, a drop of morning dew like a teardrop escaping the virgin petals. *Here he is taking his time.*

Her thigh; the maiden warrior in repose, a bow strung across her back. *Here he makes the sounds that lovers make, as if she is willing, as if she were asked.*

Her stomach where the serpent, newly burned and scabbing, wraps its length, its narrowing tail coming to rest just above her pelvis. *Here has one more place to use the knife.*

Here he is taking everything.

Here she wishes she could die.

Here she knows that she will never forget.

She ran her hand the length of her body; swiftly moving fingers taking no notice of cones.

Here is the next place where she will cut him away. Then here, and here, and here.

The first time her mother caught her cutting, she fell apart, a fit reminiscent of the time she had been caught sneaking back into the house after curfew. "It's over," her mother screamed at her, fat, angry tears swelling up in her eyes. "You don't have to relive it every night!"

And though she knew her mother meant well, still, it was a stupid thing to say. She remembers turning away, looking beyond her mother to the bay window and out onto the garden where the roses and lilies were in full bloom; Stella D Oro, Sweet Grapette. It would have been June.

"Stop trying to match his pain," her mother commanded, her voice caught in a tricky navigation between begging and commanding.

That's when she had to laugh. "Like I ever could," she replied, a little too quickly and much too honestly. Almost instantly, she felt her mother's hand land hard across her face, but she didn't mind, knowing that her anger had to settle somewhere. It was a complicated arrangement, mother and daughter both playing the victim and anyway, compared to the rest, it was a drop in the bucket.

Stream of consciousness art. The linear places in her mind. Now she knew what Roy's art must look like; a snapshot of an unforgettable, unfortunate trip beginning in a parking garage, a journey whose length would never end as long as there was skin to cut and paint with which to cover the wounded places left behind.

Roy was right, the possibilities were endless.

When the phone rang the next morning she was ready, a mug of coffee in one hand, the cordless receiver in the other.

"Good morning!" May I speak to the person who takes care of your Internet and cable needs?"

"They don't live here anymore. I can give you their number in Florida if you want," she replied, as if reading from a transcript taken from their earlier interaction.

"Florida huh? Sounds like somebody decided they couldn't make it through another Michigan winter."

"Yep."

"Well, as per our discussion yesterday morning, I must know, did you go out and buy a TV or a computer so that I can sell you an Internet and Cable bundling package?"

"No. No I did not."

"Good, what do you want to talk about then?"

She bit down on her lip. "I'm a bit rusty in the conversation department."

"I get it. Small talk got you down?"

She thought back to her last year in grad school, the time just before the attack when she was serving as the student chair of the hospitality committee, a position requiring much talk about very little with people who thought of themselves as nothing short of minor deities. Small talk had been easy then, required even, but like most things unpracticed and unvalued, had ceased to exist.

"Yea. I was thinking about you. About your art," she said, getting right to it.

"Really? My art? Cool. What do you want to know?"

She heard yelling from outside and walked over to the window. The children were out again, this time engaged in an all out war. The smallest of the four had lost her footing and fallen, an event prompting the others to join forces and pummel their sister with snow. Ignoring the onslaught, the little girl flipped over onto her back, fanning her arms and legs until the snow beneath her took on the shape of a snow angel. Her siblings, discouraged by her appropriate lack of fear, quickly relented, leaving her there on the ground before continuing the battle around the corner of their yard out of view.

"Hello? You still there?"

"Yea," she said, turning from the window. "I want you to give me a specific example of one of your paintings."

"Specific example? You mean, what is actually painted on the canvas?"

"Yes. Please."

"Hmm. Okay, got it. The one I'm working on now is called, *The gift of the Magpie*. Get it? It's a play on the O'Henry story, "The gift of the Magi." You know it?"

"Yea, I know it," she said, bringing the coffee to her lips, but finding it had chilled beyond the point of enjoyment, turned to set it on the ledge of the window. The children were back in sight now dragging each other around the yard on brightly colored toboggans, their game having changed from militaristic to one of transportation.

"So, anyway, I read somewhere about the Magpie being one of the only animals in the world that can recognize itself in a mirror and that's where I got the idea for the story. But obviously, I'm not a writer, I'm a painter. I tell my stories on canvas instead of on paper."

"I see how that could be linear, the progression of a story and all that, but what about it being stream of conscious?"

"Ah, you remembered. I'm impressed. Let me describe the way I've set it up. At the bottom of the canvas is a bunch of seemingly random objects; a tricycle with a flat tire, a crying baby, a burned out house, an unstamped postcard. Just above those are more objects, things that are obviously mundane, but they're still important, like a hamburger with a bite out of it, a bill from the electric company, a urinal-things that have become so ingrained into our everyday vernacular, we no longer recognize them as special.

In the center of the canvas is a man, his back to the viewer. All around him, the objects are repeated, only this time smaller in scale and in triplicate. They surround him, like a haze. Still with me?"

She said that she was.

"Now we get to the top half of the canvas, where we see the Magpie. He's hovers in mid-air, like a helicopter, holding two identical mirrored doors with his feet. Both mirrors show the man, but the images reflected are completely different. In the first mirror, the objects have become part of him, completely covering his skin, and he wears them like clothing. But in the second mirror, we see that the man is naked, completely free, no objects at all."

Her head began to spin. "Let me get this straight. The first set of objects are his past. They have the ability to influence his future, but don't necessarily. The mundane things are part of his present life; they're like everyday obligations. They aren't traumatic or impressionable in the same way as the first group of objects, but they're still important because, they too, influence his thinking and his ability to choose?"

"Correct."

"The mirrored doors are choices; different paths to take. In one mirror, he's unaffected by his past and his everyday obligations, and in the other, he's literally covered in them, unable to even get out from under their weight. Which path he takes is dependent on the way he views himself? And, the choice is deliberate?"

"You got it."

She could hear applause in the background, then the beginning of a round of, "Happy Birthday to You!"

"But, here's the problem," she said. "Maybe none of his experiences matter, past or present, conscious or unconscious, because it's not up to him anyway."

"Oh yea? Then who's it up to?" Roy asked.

"The Magpie. He's the omnipresent being, right? And maybe consciousness is an illusion, a cheap trick given to us by the giant puppet master Magpie in the sky, just so we can feel like we have some control over our own lives when in truth, in reality, he's been pulling the strings all along and always will, because we have no actual say over our own lives, whatsoever."

"Wow, that's really fatalistic," he said, laughing.

"Yea," she agreed, making no attempt to deny it.

"Look, that part doesn't concern me. I don't feel like it's my job to answer every question someone might have about the mysteries of life. Why did something happen-why didn't it? Who's in charge- who isn't? Is *anyone* in charge? I don't care about any of that. What interests me is the journey, not the beginning of it or even the end. What is tangible, what is real, what is happening now. The rest of that stuff, what you asked about the narrator, I can only guess. I don't know myself. I suppose that's part of my personal journey."

"So, you don't care if there's something out there in the universe making things happen to us, or on our behalf?"

"Sure, I care a great deal. I think about it a lot, but I'll never be able to prove it one way or another."

She heard a faint click come over the line. "What was that?" she asked.

"Remember, my cynical friend, these calls are on a timer. That's my one minute count down until this call is dropped. The system is designed for you, the potential customer to let me know if you're interested in ordering our services, and if that's the case, I transfer you to sales and get a commission, or if you're not, which is usually the case, you hang up in my face and the computer dials the next number on my list and I get to start my hook all over again- *Good morning! May I speak to the person who takes care of your Internet and cable needs?"*

She felt time slipping away like water through an open hand.

"But the Magpie. If you truly don't know if someone is in charge of the world then why did you paint him holding the mirrored doors? You could have just as easily painted them floating in mid-air."

"Man, you're really making me think about this, huh? Maybe that's part of my subconscious, I don't know. Truth is, Magpies are just really cool birds. They 're strong and they can carry a lot of weight. I once saw one holding a lady's purse in its beak as it flew, like the weight of the bag was nothing at all. I like them. That's all I'm willing to admit."

Across the street the children's mother stood on the stoop, calling them in for lunch. Reluctantly they conceded, stopping to retrieve their left over arsenal of snowballs and in rapid succession, unloading them against the other as they went.

"Do you think you might purchase a TV or computer by tomorrow?" Roy asked.

"Yes," she answered, hurling her answer into the phone with the same urgency as that of the snowball throwing children, just one slender moment before the line went dead.

The parking lot at the electronics store was being cleared of its snow, so she parked next door at the market, finding her way back by way of a series of adjoining sidewalks well placed in the path of the sun, last nights snow having already melted away.

She went directly to the laptops where within seconds of scanning the prices, determined new computers to be twice as expensive as she had imagined, her fingers, as if for proof, tracing the bar codes fixed on the shelf below each model; high ranking numbers revealing the steep price of memory.

"They've really gone up," she said to the salesman assisting with her selection.

"When was the last time you bought one?" he asked.

"Three years ago, in grad school."

"Time to upgrade. Technology has improved a lot in the last three years."

He walked her through the features of each model, but in the end she picked the one with the most colorful box, the deep magentas and reds of the graphics reminding her of the flashing neon sign perched above the door of tattoo parlor.

Anything else?" he asked, placing the box, *This side up*, in the cart.

"A TV."

"You need us to hook you up with an Internet and cable provider? We've got some really great bundling deals going on right now."

"No, no thanks. I already have someone in mind," she said smiling at the salesman as he led her down an alley of televisions all tuned to CNN; exact images reflecting back onto themselves like in a hall of mirrors.

"So what did you study in grad school?" the salesman asked.

"Behavioral economics," she answered, stopping in front of a twenty-six inch model sporting a thirty percent discount sticker mounted to its front.

"Behavioral economics," he repeated. "What do you do with that?"

It was the second time she'd smiled in thirty seconds. She liked it. "Not a thing, not one single thing."

The phone rang right on time. She sprang for the receiver.

"I bought a computer and a television!" she said, trying her best to control the excitement in her voice while at the same time sounding flirty. Did she sound flirty? She hoped so, but no *too* flirty.

"That's great honey, but good morning." It was her mother. She glanced across to the clock; ten thirty exactly. If she didn't get her mother off the phone quickly, she would miss Roy's call.

"Mom, can I call you back?"

"Sorry honey, no. I'm in between surgeries and the next one is about to start. I just wanted to check on you while I had a minute."

"I'm sorry Mom, but I'm expecting a phone call."

"Yes, I gathered. Something to do with the computer and television?"

Ten thirty-one. Crap.

"Mom, then can you call me back?"

"I'll try honey, but you know, I never know how long these surgeries are going to last, so I can't say exactly when it will be. That's the business of cutting, I suppose. Unpredictable."

In the background she could hear the sounds that make a hospital impossible to conceal; visitors asking for directions at the nurses station, the low mumblings of doctors reading notes into recorders, orderlies telling jokes.

"Whenever is fine. I love you. Tell daddy I love him too."

"I'll tell him when I see him. He's in surgery too. But I have to say, you're certainly in a good mood. Is it the new computer? I didn't think you cared that much. Oh my gosh, does this mean you're going back to school?"

She shook her head in amazement. It was only her mother who could make that leap.

"Mom, we'll talk later. Bye." Like it was an Olympic sport whose outcome was determined by speed, she returned the receiver to the hook, her eyes then racing to the scorekeeper on the wall. Ten thirty-four. She had missed the call.

She spent the better part of the afternoon on the phone with the automated operator of Roy's company.

"Dial one if you know your party's extension. If you don't know your party's extension, stay on the line and the operator will assist you in the order your call was received."

That last part never happened, the operator proving to be a phantom, a ghost, a tease. After waiting for exactly ten minutes for human intervention the line would simply go dead. Ten minutes. Ten minutes, times twenty attempts; exactly two-hundred minutes of wasted time. Like her mother on the phone, she began to think in terms of theory: Loss Aversion, Framing Effect, Prospect Theory, Cognitive Bias. She settled on Loss Aversion. Simply, losses hurt more than gains feel good.

Why had she put herself in this position? Roy had never been hers, instead just a voice coming in over a phone set to a timer, her parent's telephone number selected by the computer charged with maintaining the entirely random system. Something had to be yours in order for it to be taken away and obviously, he wasn't. The idea that she found herself missing him was utterly ridiculous, especially since, other than him being a struggling artist, she knew nothing about him. Was he straight, gay, married, unable to commit? Tall, short, fat, blond, dark, Native American, Chinese? Interested in her, even a little bit?

Inevitably those questions would have come up, maybe even today had she gotten her ten minutes with him. And if so, it would have come to this, because it always did; Roy not being able to help himself, but asking her, what did she look like? It's only natural that he would have wanted to know. What would she have told him? That she was of average height and build, a brunette who hadn't cut her hair in years, even though her mother had literally begged her to. Hazel eyes, and oh, by the way, incidentally, not that it surely matters because it's hardly worth mentioning at all, but painted in tattoos, most of the completely nonsensical variety, from shoulders to the tops of her feet, and cut, all the places in between.

Would she have told him that in the morning her face wore an expression of only moderate sadness but by the afternoon, when she became frantic and desperate, her appearance would morph into that of a junkie needing a fix. And that's when she would cut. When the sun went down over the landscape and the children across the street were forced back inside to the firelight of their home. When her parent's house became like the tension filled waiting room of a hospital, she would get to the business of cutting, carving away the unwanted memories her attacker left behind.

Loss Aversion. Losses hurt more than gains feel good. It wouldn't have been worth it, anyway. Probably not.

The snow fell in drifts as she pulled her father's car into the parking lot of the tattoo parlor. Short of one other vehicle, a beat-up, gray Honda whose bumper was plastered in stickers, the place was empty. Not a big surprise, with both the snow and the holidays. Through the plate glass window she could see Rock-n-Roll, his long dark hair gathered from the nape of his neck and pulled back in a pony tail.

"Happy white, almost Christmas," he greeted her, as she walked in the door.

Maybe it was the almost thing with Roy, or maybe, because Christmas was just days away and soon she would be trading the Currier and Ives landscape of Michigan for the sun drenched beaches of Florida, but good grief, this guy, this Rock-n-Roll character, was certainly good-looking.

Long hair pulled back away from his face revealing high,

ethnic looking cheekbones, chin covered in days-worth of stubble. Good-looking.

Multiple piercings; eyebrows, ears, who knows where else. Tats, sticking out past the collar of his tight-fitting t-shirt. Good-looking.

Definitely not the kind of guy you brought home to meet your two doctor parents. She remembered enough of her rebellious high school self to know that possibly, that information might make him appear even better looking than he actually was. Whatever. She didn't care. Good-looking.

And even though, for God's sake, he had chosen Rock-n-Roll to go by professionally, he was still ridiculously good-looking.

Again, maybe she was a victim of the almost thing, or of the romance of the season, the twinkling snow falling from the sky and dancing in illumination before the glow of the street lights, but good grief, Rock-n-Roll was good-looking. Why hadn't she noticed this before? Incredulously, she began to miss him, her visits to the parlor now feeling numbered like days marked from a calender.

She smiled a greeting then began her walk among the flash, stopping ever so often to touch a design before moving on to another, almost always returning to the one she'd just held before moving on again. As she wandered through the art, she thought of Roy's campaign, of his commitment to the importance of progression, and so decided to pick a design from which she could glean a story, a story whose origin past was not evident but whose future seemed likely. A knight in pursuit of a dragon caught her eye. She leaned in closer to examine the title and signature at the bottom. *Facing the*

Demon by Rock-n-Roll. She took the paper from the wall.

"Let's do this one," she told him, holding up the design.

"Excellent," he beamed. "I just finished drawing that one an hour ago. Let's go back to my room."

She followed him to the back of the building to his station. Before the tattoo artists had moved in, the building had been the home to a hair salon and was in many ways, still set up as such. Beside the coat rack where Rock-n-Roll kept his jacket hung stood a bonnet hair dryer, a life sized stuffed University of Michigan wolverine sitting under the dome stuck in a perpetual state of drying. And a barbers chair, having once been in the center of the room, had been moved into the corner in favor of a tattoo bed on which clients seeking ink for their more private places spread out, revealing themselves in more longitudinal comfort.

She choose the table over the chair.

"I can guess, but where we gonna put this one?" he asked, sitting opposite her in the barber's chair.

She pulled her skirt up to reveal the new wounds she'd carved into the upper portion of her thigh. She hadn't worn her wool tights, the idea of having to pull them down in front of him keeping them confined to a drawer at home.

"Here."

He rose slowly from the chair, his eyes never leaving the damage to her leg as he traveled the short distance between them.

"Hot damn, girl. Hot damn." With his fingers he drew circles around the cuts even though the wounds themselves were not circular at all but instead were winding and jagged, like the disconnected tributaries of a dying river, his hands retreating only when he had gotten a feel for the broken geography of her leg. He left her at the table, turning his attention to a shelf across the room housing his paints.

"Can we cover it?" she asked. He had his back to her now, efficient hands working through the row of colors. Suddenly, he turned back to her, hands full of vermilion.

"Okay, I'm sorry. But, why do you keep doing this to yourself? I mean, it's none of my business, but damn, what's so wrong?"

She felt the ambush most in the crimson blushing of her cheeks. She had no idea how to answer or even if she should, but it didn't matter; he wasn't done.

"I mean, you are so pretty and you drive that nice car and you're sweet, I can tell that you are, even though you don't say much, I get that you're a good person. And for whatever reason, you come to me only, every time, expecting me to fix you, but I can't. I can't keep doing it anymore. I'm afraid that by covering up your scars, I'm only encouraging you to cut and I really, really, don't want to be any part of that."

He waited for her to jump into the conversation, to take up for herself, to tell him to go to Hell, anything, but when she didn't, he continued with his speech.

"I don't get it, man. I've always thought that the beginning and the end of a person's personal journey weren't important, but that the journey itself was the essential part. But now, here's you, blowing my theory apart, because something so obviously substantial happened to you that it started you down this path. It was important, way important. And that's cool, I understand that it was deep. But here's why I'm afraid. I'm afraid that some day I won't see you anymore and it's because you've cut yourself so deep that every drop of paint in this whole shop won't be enough to fix you."

He threw himself onto the seat of the blower, forcing the wolverine to the floor. For a while no one said anything; she could hear the clock ticking on the wall, and a siren going off somewhere further down the street. In the self-imposed silence of the room, the sounds seemed to amplify, the tacit urgencies fixed to the noises only adding to her already heightened state of anxiety. She wanted to get down from the table, to run out the front door of the parlor, forever leaving Rock-n-Roll behind, but for the life of her, couldn't imagine how to do it.

"I'm sorry," he finally said, looking up at the ceiling. "I'm having a bad day. I don't mean to take it out on you. I was looking forward to something that didn't happen and thanks to the giant computer that runs my life five days a week from eight to five, never will." He stopped here and paused, momentarily closing his eyes before getting back into it. "Plus, I'm working on a painting, that after talking to this girl that I don't even really know, I now realize may be complete bullshit and it probably doesn't matter because no one will ever want to buy it anyway, and I'll be stuck working here forever in this tattoo parlor at night and in a call center during the day, trying to sell Internet bundling packages to people who wished more than anything, they hadn't answered their phones."

She knew this was the part of the conversation in which she should attempt to comfort him by interjecting an opinion or personal philosophy, but because she was busy working the math, didn't offer either.

"I'm really sorry," he repeated, thumping the bottles of paints in an indiscernible rhythm against his leg. "I think I'm having an existential crisis. Sometimes I just get so sick of the theoretical empire in my mind that I don't know what to do. *Theories*-they're all bullshit. Know what I mean?"

She did.

"Ask me if I bought a TV and a computer?" She was surprised at how easily the words rolled from her tongue after having been silent for so long.

"What?" he asked, his confusion so apparent, so delicious, that she almost laughed.

"Ask me. Go ahead."

Now it was his turn to work the impossible equation of their meeting. Had he been a character in a cartoon, a light bulb, yellow and burning brightly would have appeared above his head illuminating him like a halo does an angel.

"Did you, by chance, buy a TV or a computer?" He dropped the paints to the floor, bringing the leg music to an end.

"Yes, I did." She lowered her skirt, returning the length to her knee.

She stood up from the table and he from the blower and they met in the middle of the room where the barber's chair had once been fastened, a round ring of linoleum still missing and the sub-floor showing through. She started at the beginning. How it all began in a campus parking garage only a month before graduation; one moment of focus lost in order to pick up dropped keys.

She walked him down the path of her skin, starting with the scar on her shoulder where her attacker had first used the knife; a temporary layover before making his way to her heart. She explained how the man took his time with her, in a way, forever making her his. How in different ways he had touched her all over, taking special care to leave no part of her body unspoiled.

She swore to Roy that she tried, truly she had, but some days she couldn't help but to try to cut this man's memory away.

It was then that she took his hand and placing it under her skirt, asked him to touch her. He protested but she insisted, gently guiding his fingers along the secret trail leading to the final place where the man had used his the knife. She slid her underwear to the side, telling him there were three spots where the attacker had cut her, two on the outside, but the last, hidden within. She steered him to the first and then the second but when he began to pull his hand away before finding the third she stopped him, telling him that it was important that he continue on. He nodded and she, turning her face away from his, stared out the window, letting him finish his work in private. On the street a car went by slowly, its headlights cutting a zig-zag pattern across the snow.

When Roy's hand came to a stop, she told him of the children across the street, about the snow ball wars they waged, and of the little girl whose spirit could not be broken. She told him how she would never have any children of her own, her doctors were sure, all because of that one horrible night in the parking garage. How unfair, she mused, the choice of a family being taken away long before she had even begun to explore the possibility of wanting one.

She finished with a promise; that she would never cut through one of his tattoos, she liked them too much, how the ink decorated the canvas of her skin in a way that she had chosen, not in a way that had been chosen for her. The skin beneath them would be safe, always.

It was then that Roy went to work, gathering paints from the shelves, opening drawers and pulling out brushes, slowly removing her clothes and folding them neatly, placing the pile on the seat of the blower where the wolverine could keep watch.

He started with a Geisha on her hip. Shy and reserved the girl looked out from an open fan, a kiss of a smile peaking out past the curvature of the instrument. Next a butterfly, painted in the deepest of blues, wings spreading across the width of her back like a tide breaching land. Across her breasts a progression of roses grew; bud to blossom, blossom to hip, thorn yielding a single drop of blood.

An orchid, a daisy, a tongue-in-cheek interpretation of the tooth fairy.

A unicorn, a shamrock, a Leatherback sea turtle, a fox emerging from its den. Mario, Luigi, Princess Peach. All images from the linear places of his mind.

When the canvas of her skin could hold no more he led her to the mirror hanging on the door. She placed her hand upon the painted face of the girl standing there. She was beautiful, like a rainbow out of place, one you don't expect to see because conditions aren't exactly right.

"It's no good," she whispered. "They'll all just wash away."

"Let them," he replied. "I will paint you again and again."

She turned to face him, the azure wings across her back appearing in the mirror as those of a hovering angel.

"My name is Alice," she said extending her hand, as if

meeting for the first time.

"Well, nice to me you, Alice," Roy said, taking her hand. "Alice," he repeated. "That suits you."

Outside the snow kept falling, the lights from the street lamps reflecting on the glistening ground and illuminating all earthly things, images appearing in doubles, as if they too were being seen in a mirror. Above the door of the parlor the neon sign flashed to life, letters pulsing together like a collection of heartbeats; *Magpie Tattoos*, shining like an emblem out into the night, across the magnificent wonderland of snow.

Banshee

There's a ghost in the Walmart. Aisle Three. Automotives.

When Maurice Dollarwhip took a box down from the shelf to discern the country of origin, there she was, poking her head out from the between the cans of Pennzoil and screaming her head off. Maurice fainted dead away landing on the floor, limbs out, spread eagle style every which-a-way.

It took two managers and a janitor to revive him and when he finally did come to, he said he was never coming to the Walmart again, *as long as he lived.*

"Because of the ghost?" Byron, the meat department manager wanted to know.

"That," said Maurice, "and that the lines at the registers are way too long, because there are never enough checkers."

The specter woman was last seen hanging out between the spark plugs and a life size cardboard cutout of Dale

Earnhardt Junior, his frozen likeness forever extolling the benefits of Armor All. Mr. Dollarwhip was last seen heading over to the meat department with Byron, the promise of a complimentary ham ushering him along.

This is why the Walmart Corporation, southwest regional division, which includes most of Texas, all of Oklahoma and the western quarter of Arkansas, has hired a psychic. At first, they sent us a board certified paranormal investigator to assist in the removal of our ghost, but that only made matters worse, exacerbating the wayward spirit to a level of hysteria which I had not been unlucky enough to experience since before Black Friday became a thing.

I'm sure this paranormal investigator had the best of intentions, but I don't mind telling you, that no one, and I repeat, no one, dead or alive, likes being told what to do. It goes against our very nature! So, when the P.I. commanded the spirit to "get out of the Walmart," *and* "go back to where you came from," I could tell simply by the look on that spooks face that she had no intention of doing so.

Fast as lightning, she swooped out from behind the rack of feminine hygiene products she was busy haunting, positioned herself directly in front of that poor fool's face, then forcing his mouth open with her dead, bony fingers, threw up all in there. Disgusting. The entire store smelled like fish for two weeks.

For days afterwards she roamed the aisles making trouble; screaming her freaking head off and grabbing Jello pudding cups right out of peoples carts, ferociously hurling them up against the walls with a velocity any fast ball throwing pitcher would envy. Before long, we couldn't even keep that product in stock! Tensions surrounding the situation were at an all time high.

"That ghost is literally taking food out of my baby's mouth!" one woman complained as her child stood in the basket of her shopping cart stomping his little feet and wailing a spontaneous lament over the afore mentioned product.

"Yes, ma'am," Byron consoled. "Would you like a complimentary ham?"

One of our greeters, Darlene, who lives in a haunted trailer park down on the old highway, suggested perhaps the ghost was confused, or maybe desperate to communicate with someone who understood the spiritual realm better than Byron the meat manager and that she personally, had had real good luck with a woman named Inez Cruz.

Inez Cruz was a bit of a local legend. A business woman of varied professional interest, Inez operated a beauty parlor, finishing school *and* a psychic reading room out of the A-frame building that once served as the office of the KOA Campground until it, like most of the businesses on that side of town, went belly up.

The Walmart used to be over on that side of town too, but moved when the interstate expanded in the opposite direction. Personally, I liked the old store better. It was smaller and folks could find things more easily and plus, my commute to work was shorter as I live just a few blocks from there. On nice days, I would walk to work, leaving a few minutes early so that I could window shop at the stores on Main Street. But now, most of those businesses are gone and with the new store being so far away, that kind of commute is no longer an option.

But Byron didn't like the idea of Inez and put off calling her, even after he'd gotten permission from corporate for the hire. He'd heard strange things about her, things that went against the very way he was raised. Rumors, such as her refusal to use toothpaste as well as operating a blog claiming that Fluoride was a conspiracy perpetrated upon the American people by the American Academy of Dentist in partnership with the United States Government, and that she did not have a church home, choosing instead to spend her Sunday morning worship time with the shut-ins at Serenity Gardens Nursing Facility, performing readings and setting hair.

But perhaps her greatest sin came about during a special promotion here in the store when Byron offered Inez a sample of ham and flatly, she turned him down.

"I do not care for the concept of ham," she told Byron sympathetically, as if ham were a disease from which Byron might be cured. The list went on and on.

So instead of Inez, Byron brought in a Choctaw medicine woman, a Catholic priest, and a Rabi. Where he found that last one I don't know.

The medicine woman took one look at the ghost before declaring she was ready for the ham she'd been promised. "Not one of ours," we heard her say as she headed out the front door pushing an enormous spiral cut in a cart to her car.

And while the priest insisted upon throwing holy water at the tortured soul, an action producing no affect what-so-ever, it was the Rabi who elicited the most positive response out of the three. Under his tutelage the ghost sat quietly, listening intently as he read aloud the story of Abraham and Sara from the Chumash.

After spending the better part of an hour with our ghost, the Rabi declared the situation to be at an in-pass, saying that he felt there to be a language barrier between the two, but all the same, thanking Byron very much for the opportunity to preach to a good listener as he very rarely encountered such a person these days.

Bryon was visibly disappointed, but at least had the good sense not to offer the man a ham.

After so many failures, Byron was forced to call Inez. She agreed to take the case and promised to be at the store by four thirty that afternoon. The call was placed at four. Five minutes later she walked into the Walmart. To this day, I have no idea how she got here that fast.

Inez was a peculiar person from the get go. I guess the first thing I noticed about her was that on her shoulder sat a parrot enjoying a confident state of repose, the kind of bird you might see keeping company with the captain of a pirate ship. Sadly, this particular bird did not offer any words, but instead spent his time lazily eyeing the group of spectators who had gathered to greet the psychic. Miss Flo, from jewelry, who confessed to owning a talking parrot as a child, refused to let the bird be, aligning her face with that of the animal and commanding that it try to say something! Anything! But especially, *Flo!*

After a couple of minutes the bird put a stop to the bullying by grabbing hold of Flo's nose and twisting it sideways. Soon thereafter, specialized bargaining began and eventually a trade was made; Flo's nose for a Cheez-It. I think it is safe to say that both parties were pleased with the outcome of what was quickly becoming a rather uncomfortable situation.

By merely looking, I could not attain the genealogical background of Ms. Cruz's people as she looked a little bit like everything as well as a whole lot of nothing. Her skin revealed it self to be neither light nor dark, but of medium tone. Her eyes, sitting high upon the frame of her face were set widely apart; but while one was blue, the other could only be described as having the color likeness of a newly minted copper penny, and possessing that same luminescence as well.

Her nose was flat, her neck long and elegant. Her chin, which she held up proudly as she walked, strong and square.

Her age? I could not begin to guess.

Now to Ms. Inez Cruz's clothing. I found it strange that she wore a full length ball gown, one with so daring a neckline and sleeveless as well, especially being that we were smack dab in the middle of the coldest January on record, but really, who am I to judge? I am not gifted with any degree of psychic ability and therefore could not tell you the proper uniform for dressing a person with talents such as seeing into the future, locating disenfranchised loved ones, or banishing ghosts from the Pawnee, Oklahoma Walmart. Perhaps, dressed in formal attire is always the way the clairvoyant present themselves to strangers.

Oh, and I do believe she was wearing a wig as her hair did appear to be crooked. Plus, it was the color of Watermelon flavored Kool-Aid, and not particularly of hair.

Did I mention she wore long, silken gloves ending at the elbow but housed her feet in camouflaged combat boots caked in mud? Or that just above her lip she had drawn a beauty mark using what could have only been a felt tip pen, the proper drying time unobserved and the token smeared well up into the cavern of her nostril? Well, she did-she really did!

But even though she was funny looking as all get out, I could tell she had a real big heart. She started off the psychic session by taking up a collection for the local animal shelter, (thirty six dollars and fourteen cents!) then followed up that act of kindness by showing us a cat video on the You Tube channel of her smart phone.

After it was over, she confessed that she had a vested interest in that particular video, as the musical genius shown there playing the piano was none other than her very own Mr. Pussykins. Byron made a big show of saying that Mr. Pussykins's musical capabilities were nothing short of astounding and asked Inez if she had taught the cat to play. She assured us that she had not and that the cat, having learned the skill himself, was a virtuoso in his own right.

The song Mr. Pussykins performed was, "Twinkle, Twinkle Little Star." Not too shabby for a cat.

After everyone displayed the proper amount of amazement, Inez said that she was ready to get to work, so we led her over to the automotive department where the ghost had last been seen, but of course when we got there our spook was no where to be found.

Isn't that just always the way? When you're looking for a ghost, you can't ever find one.

Inez told us not to worry, she would locate our specter. She took off down the aisle, the train of her gown catching Mr. Earnhardt Junior's foot as she turned the corner, dragging him along.

It didn't take Inez long to find our ghost; she was hiding

inside the dairy case, squeezed in between the regular and the almond milk. Right away I could tell she was more put out than usual.

Her hair had turned to snakes, the serpents pulsing and undulating slowly back and forth like the pan caught ripples of a drip, and her skin, normally a pale, glowing white during tranquil times, had turned an ashen shade of gray; both unmistakable signs marking the beginning of a real bad experience for any one crossing her path.

These strange anomalies only happened when our ghost was at her worst; throwing fluorescent light tubes across the store, jumping out from the children's coat displays in hopes of terrifying the most vulnerable of customers or worst of all, screaming at the top of her lungs for minutes on end, a sound shriller and more disturbing than that of any dog whistle ever blown on earth.

A knowing murmur went through the crowd; Miss Flo headed back to jewelry.

Inez stood there observing our ghost through the glass and shaking her head; her way of expertly conveying much displeasure at the situation. When Byron asked what was wrong, Inez shook her head even harder.

"I am not excited *at all* that our spirit is a banshee, they can be so hard to work with," she confided as the parrot crossed the naked skin of her shoulders to perch on the other side. "I think you all better get back."

There was a shuffling of feet as our group scooted over to the sanctity of the frozen pizza section. Inez opened the door to the cooler. Collectively, we held our breath.

I don't know what I expected exactly. A scene from *The*

Exorcist? Or *Carrie* maybe? Spinning heads or blood like rain dripping down from the top of the coolers? Neither one happened. What did happen was this: Inez, reaching into the cooler, gently taking the hand of the banshee, and greeting her warmly in a language none of us could understand.

The banshee's eyes got wide as dinner plates and it sounded to me as though she were answering the psychic using the same confounding vernacular. They went back and forth like this for a time and after a while it became obvious that they truly were communicating. For the first time ever, our banshee smiled, displaying a set of perfect teeth none us had ever been privy to seeing. Pretty soon the two of them were giggling like they were old friends. I swear, I think I even heard that parrot laugh!

Byron said he thought that based on the rhythm and timing of their conversation, they must be telling knock-knock jokes.

A woman walked by wearing a full length fur coat and without even turning around, Inez told Byron that the woman was shoplifting.

"Inside that murderous shroud you will find exactly three boxes of Lipton Cup-A-Soup-French Onion flavor-a bottle of store brand aspirin, and a package of Dr. Scholl's shoe inserts, women's size nine to eleven."

Bryon took off after the woman saying that he couldn't imagine why anyone on earth would shoplift Lipton's Cup-A-Soup but that he could certainly understand the inserts. After a few minutes he was back wanting to know what he'd missed.

Now, by this point, Irene was covered in chill bumps from standing there so long in the open door of the cooler, so when the banshee motioned that she was willing to come out, the psychic gladly accepted the offer. We followed the two of them over to the snack bar where Byron bought them both a hot chocolate that sadly, when she attempted to drink it, went clean through the banshee, spilling out all over the floor. But Inez, being a solid object and all, had better luck keeping hers down, at times even sharing with her bird.

Who knew that a parrot could drink from a straw? Incredible!

The new friends sat across from each other in the booth positioned directly underneath the poster proclaiming the good news that Revereware was, *still made in the USA!* Their hands entwined like sisters, they took on each other's mannerisms; Inez tapping her foot when the Banshee did, the Banshee smoothing a snake away from her face each time Inez redirected her own curls.

Every once in a while Inez would forget to respond to the banshee's chinwag using the language common between them.

"Yes, I see. It does sound as though *you were* invited," and "No, you're right, it is a terrible burden to bear."

But this breach didn't seem to slow down the rate at which the banshee told her story. If there's one thing I've learned over the years, it's that sometimes it doesn't matter all that much if you get a response when you're venting because mainly, you just want to let off the steam.

It was by piecing together these few uncoded, scattered bits from their conversation that we formed an understanding of why the banshee was in the Pawnee, Oklahoma Walmart in the first place. Number one, apparently someone had invited her and number two, she'd been here a long time, but none of us had taken the time to notice. So why, after so many years of silence, had she started this aggressive campaign of torturous screaming? Because we finally *had* noticed her, that's why.

An old woman came up pushing her mostly dead looking husband in a wheel chair cart, their basket filled to the brim with diabetic supplies and water balloons. It seemed to me out of character for a diabetic to need so many water balloons, maybe a pack or two, but five? Really? But there again, who am I to judge.

Where in the world is Amy the store manager, the woman wanted to know; she had a complaint. Byron told her that Amy was out on maternity leave and asked if could he help.

The old folks answered with a hearty round of, *well, I'll be* and *isn't that nice.* Then in the spirit of competition that only sixty years of blissful marriage can so successfully produce, jockeyed so aggressively for the honor to be the first to shake Byron's hand that the wife knocked the husband out of his wheelchair seat and onto the floor. I don't know why the rush to congratulate Byron; he sure didn't have anything to do with it.

"Good Lord, Stromble," the woman scolded, "get back in the chair!"

It took four of us to lift the man and another three to hold the cart steady, the old woman, I think completely out of pure orneriness, shaking the contraption so viscously that replacing the man to the seat became a greater challenge than any of us had received training for during the company workshop entitled, *The Difficult Guest and You.*

It was like being asked to fit a two hundred and fifty pound sack of potatoes into a rotating one inch hole.

"What the heck is going on back here, anyway?" the man huffed.Byron explained that we were working on our banshee situation. The woman rolled her evil eye over the lot of us and said that it looked to be quite the group project, only she didn't say it as a compliment.

"Just ignore that banshee, that's what I do. Banshee, my foot," the crabby pants instructed.

Easy for her to say. I guarantee that old biddy has never been stocking a shelf at half past midnight when a screaming ghoul flies out at her from between the Tupperware, wrestles the price gun away, then marks -4.99-ROLL BACK PRIC-ES!-up side *her* head.

After finally getting the man situated back in the cart, Byron escorted the couple up front to the registers, because as it turns out, that's what the complaint was; no checkers.

Inez stood up from the table, took a moment to adjust herself in the top shelf department, then made the announcement. "That's it."

The banshee took off flying toward the pet food aisle, screeching the entire way there. Shortly afterward, we heard a customer scream bloody murder; our ghost was back in business.

Wanting to know what had been decided, we crowded around Inez.

"Well, nothing," she said matter-of-factly. "These problems can't be solved overnight. Takes time, and diplomacy."

We followed her to the Exit where she curtsied her goodbye, the parrot returning to its original perch as she shifted her weight.

Byron got back just in time to see the psychic step out onto the pedestrian crossing in front of the store where she was immediately mowed down by a Fed Ex truck. I bet you her wig flew twenty five feet straight up in the air. Turns out, I was right.

Later that week in the break room, Byron said that he really didn't understand it. Inez was a psychic, why hadn't she seen that coming?

We never did find her bird.

And the banshee? She's still here, and it looks like to stay.

Since we were so unsuccessful in evicting her, corporate insisted that we display a sign warning customers that our particular Walmart is haunted, an attempt I believe, to ward off the threat of a lawsuit in the event that our banshee screams somebody straight into the arms of the Grim Reaper.

Bryon went to Smith and Brothers Printing, over on the old highway, to have the notice made up, but when he got to the shop, the only sign to be had was the one hanging sideways in the window; *Sorry, out of business.*

Bent

I am the Lone Ranger.

A fiery horse with the speed of light, a cloud of dust and a hearty Hi-Yo Silver! The Lone Ranger!

I am not Tonto.

With his faithful Indian companion Tonto, the daring and resourceful masked rider of the plains led the fight for law and order in the early western United States!

I have my very own gun. Mama says-

Outside Bently, if you're going to shoot that gun.

But I just ignore her because I'm the Lone Ranger, not Bently.

Nowhere in the pages of History can one find a greater champion of justice!

Pop, pop, pop! The TV Lone Ranger has a *REAL* gun that fires *REAL* silver bullets. That's sure a heck of a lot better than what I have because what I have is a cap gun and I almost didn't even get that! Because Mama said-

No, no guns is my house. Not even toy guns.

Then Mr. Knight said-

Yes, it'll make him a man someday.

But then Mama said-

What if I don't want him to be a man someday? What if I want him to be my baby forever?

So then Mr. Knight said-

Lilith honey, you wouldn't want a baby forever, nobody would.

And that's when Mama turned on the water works. So, while everybody was distracted by all that bawling and carrying on, I took the gun up to the register and paid for it myself. Plus two boxes of extra caps. Plus a package of Twinkies. Also an eye patch in case I ever want to dress up as a pirate for Halloween. Or, if I get poked in the eye with a stick.

When the man behind the register rang me up, he looked me square in the eye and said, "Now be a good boy and promise not to aim that gun at nobody." I agreed, saying, "Yessir." He held out his hand so that we could shake on it like gentlemen, which we did, then he gave me my change. Sixty-seven cents; enough to buy one more Twinkie. I unwrapped it real fast and shoved the whole thing into my mouth before anyone could tell me differently.

But as I made that promise, I crossed my fingers behind my back because if I ever catch those darned old Cavendish boys breaking into our house again, I will aim to kill. And that, is a promise is aim to keep.

When I shoot my gun, real smoke comes out! The smoke fills the whole entire living room just like Papa Jim's cigars do on Sundays when he comes over after church, puffing and carrying on. Papa Jim is married to Mama Ruth. They are my first daddy's mama and daddy, which makes them my grandparents. Even though my first daddy left, they kept coming around so finally Mama gave up and started inviting them. She claims that by issuing an official summons, she has decreased the frequency of their visits by exactly one-hundred and twenty-seven percent, although, when I tried to work that number out mathematically on the kitchen calculator, it was impossible to rectify.

Mama Ruth has one enormous breast, but just one because a disease took the other one away. I asked her once if she missed that breast and she told me that she didn't much, but Papa Jim sure did.

When they visit, Mama Ruth always sits on the couch while Papa Jim sits in Mr. Knight's reclining chair, the one he had to have because his back hurts.

"Come sit on my lap, darlin'," Mama Ruth calls to me.

I put my head on her chest, in the place where the breast used to be and think of all the lonely places I've been before and never want to go back to: kindergarten, first grade, second grade, especially third grade. The emergency room at Pinnacle Hills Hospital. Mrs. Epson's Sunday school for boys only class, the field and the woods behind our house.

Mama Ruth holds me close, rocking me back and forth like a baby. She says stuff like-

I love you a pickle and a poke, and, *you make my big ole heart whistle.*

I don't remember of course, but Papa Jim says that Mama Ruth was the only one who could get me to quit crying when I was a baby. Mama says that's an exaggeration.

"How much of an exaggeration?" I asked one night as she was tucked the covers in tight around me, which is exactly the way I like it.

"Slight," she answered. "Just slight."

Return with us now to those thrilling days of yesteryear! From out of the past come the thundering hoof beats of the great horse Silver!

I do not have a horse, just a cat named Whiskers. Whiskers is fine as far as cats go, but she is no Silver. She gets scared when I shoot off my gun and then Mama says to leave her alone-

Whiskers is as old as the hills.

We used to have a dog named Ralph, but he bit the mailman and had to go live on a farm. I don't know which farm because no one will tell me, but I hope for his sake, it's a nice farm. One time after a day spent wandering around the county, Ralph came home with an entire Rhubarb pie! I told him, "Good boy, Ralph," because normally Rhubarb pie is my favorite, only Ralph's pie tasted gritty, like it had been dragged through the dirt and I guess technically it had but I thought it was worth a shot anyway, a sentiment Mama did not share. On a scale marking hysterical behavior, Mama would usually come in somewhere around the moderate range but that day she went off the charts, squeezing the sides of my face so forcefully that I had no choice but to spit out the piece I was working on. Then, she dragged me in and brushed my teeth with baking soda. Twice. Next came the Listerine. It was not a day for the faint of heart.

I'm pretty sure I'm not the only one who received the swift hand of justice that day. I'm almost positive Mama kicked

Ralph. I was leaned over the sink trying to recover from a years worth of hygiene when I heard him yelp, but since I didn't actually see it I can't prove it. Still, I strongly suspect.

Besides the mailman, here is a list of things that Ralph chewed up:

Mr. Knight's secret stash of money: mostly tens and twenties. This is currency that Mr. Knight keeps in a pillow case hidden under the bed in case of a natural disaster or government meltdown, both of which he professes to being inevitable.

Mama's favorite pair of dungarees: size ten, though she would point out that a size ten is technically two sizes too big for her, but that she likes her work clothes roomy.

The gas line leading from the house to the air-conditioning unit: all the grown-ups agree that one could have ended really badly and seem to enjoy talking about it from time to time.

The tires on Mr. Knight's patrol car: all four, while they were still on the car, but not while it was moving.

Lastly, the trunk of the Mulberry Tree out in the front yard. It died soon after and had to be cut down. "Way to go, Ralph the mouth," Mama said to him as we watched the tree man take it down. "You owe me three-hundred dollars, you dumb dog." Ralph's tail moved from side to side in happy position; obviously he did not understand the tone.

When the Mulberry started to fall, the tree man yelled, "Timber!" Ralph howled. Mama rolled her eyes. Mr. Knight laughed. I shot my gun up in the air. Yee haw!

The Lone Ranger rides again!

Clap clap clap, clip-o-d-clop! I gallop around the living

room on my own two feet. Horse or no horse, I can make that beautiful clip-cloppidy sound. I slap my hand on my rear, faster and faster as I pick up speed. I'm moving on! Past the funny looking cactus peppering the landscape, past the secret silver mine where my bullets are forged, past the graveyard that'll be too good a spot to bury the likes of those Cavendish boys when I finally bring them to justice and I swear that I will! No one escapes the long hand of the Lone Ranger, no one. Hi-Yo Silver! Away!

I've decided to always be the Lone Ranger, and never, ever be Bently again. Mr. Knight says that pretending is all well and good but you just can't pretend all the time. I told him that I would quit pretending if he would. That was the last thing said between us before he went into the kitchen and started slamming cabinet doors.

Mama said-

Percy, what in the world is wrong with you?

Then Mr. Knight said-

Bently, Bently is what is wrong with me.

And then Mama said-

Oh, and nothing more.

Sometimes Mr. Knight comes home from work in a real good mood and sometimes he comes home in a bad mood, but he always comes home, which Mama says is the import-ant part so be a good boy and ignore the rest.

I think there may be a reason the Lone Ranger on TV doesn't have a mother.

Anyway, it's not pretending, it's an adoption, just like what Mr. Knight did with me when he married Mama and became my second daddy. It all happened down at the courthouse and real fast, so fast that in fact, I didn't even know what *was* happening.

It was summer and I was busy sweating through three layers of clothes when the judge said, "Come forward." Mama pulled me up from my chair and brushed the hair out of my eyes. "Smile Bently, honey," she said. "Try to look happy."

"You're choking me, woman," I said in response to the placement of her hand on the back of my neck which was just a little too tight if you ask me.

The judge asked Mama and Mr. Knight a bunch of questions and to each and every one they answered, *yessir*, and the next thing I know, the judge is decrying congratulations by saying "Many felicitations young man, you just got yourself a new daddy."

I looked around to see who he was talking to and when it became obvious that there was nobody else in the courtroom of a formative age as required by the state of Arkansas for the purposes of adoption but me, I began to feel mighty peculiar; hand sweats, blurred vision, explosive diarrhea.

A man named Bailiff ushered me out of the courtroom real fast and into the bathroom. By the time I got back, Mama and Mr. Knight were having their picture taken with the judge. The judge's name turned out to be Applekraut-Judge Applekraut. Whoever heard of a name like that? Anyway, he stood between the two of them holding an official looking piece of paper in one hand and furiously shaking Mr. Knight's with the other.

"Come and have your picture made with your new daddy, young man," Judge Applekraut said motioning me over and smiling like a cat that had just figured out how to open up the canary cage.

"Smile honey," Mama said again, only this time she wasn't using her real smile, but her fake one, the one that she reserves for short-changing store clerks and for Mama Ruth when she asks all those questions that are none of her business.

After the court reporter finished taking the picture we all hugged, right there in the courtroom with everybody watching. Because Mama said we had to. Also, Mama made me wear a Sunday school suit, and it wasn't even Sunday! With a tie. And a real one-not even a clip on! Like a noose, I can still feel it pinching around my neck.

Nobody asked me about any of it.

Mama framed the certificate and to this very day it sits atop the buffet in the dining room. It's a real fancy looking thing, the words, *Certificate of Adoption*, written across the top in a hoity-toity, puffed-up script. I used to enjoy sticking my fingernail into the letters in an attempt to deflate them, but Mama put a stop to that by giving me a lecture, the basis of which pretty much hinged on the idea that poking letters on adoption certificates was paramount to denouncing the whole adoption process world wide, no exceptions, then taking the certificate downtown to *The Hang It Up!* and having it framed.

Mama Ruth says that the letters on the certificate are embossed. She says "embossed," like it's a dirty word. *Em-bossed*. She also said it was gonna be a real surprise, when Dean, that's my first daddy, comes back home and finds that Mama has gone out and gotten me a new daddy, a statement to which Mama said, "Oh, it'll be a real surprise all right-son of a bitch."

Painted on the adoption certificate is an enormous tree

comprised almost entirely of branches whose length spreads and twirls around the page in a way that I find downright menacing. If I hang my head to the side and look at it while holding one eye in a squint, I swear it looks like those limbs are reaching for me! I told Whiskers all about it one night while we were under the covers reading, "The Hero's Guide to Being an Outlaw," but she didn't seem to care. If Ralph hadda been there, I'm pretty sure he would have at least wagged his tail.

Each maniacal branch eventually straightens out to form a blank line where you are instructed to "record your family history," (those exact words are printed below each branch). This is where Judge Applekraut had Mama and Mr. Knight sign their names. And while their John Hancock's sit high on the top branches getting all the glory, my name is written down below where it's almost completely hidden in what looks like some sort of underbrush. Mama says that's just the way the certificate was designed and it doesn't mean anything and to try to look past it and to that I say, fine, sure; where to?

Below that you'll find six more blank lines. "When your family grows your tree can too!" (printed on the certificate as well).

Also, written on the back of the certificate, but that can no longer be seen since mama framed it-

Water your tree with love and watch it grow
Order additional branches at your leisure, twenty four hours a
day at familytreematters.com
and
Printed on recycled paper so that a real tree didn't have to die

for your tree

And that is how Mr. Knight became my new daddy. So, if it's that easy for Mr. Knight to adopt me, just a trip to the courthouse and a signed piece of paper with a scary tree drawn all over it, then why can't I adopt The Lone Ranger? Seems fair enough to me.

To prove my point, I made myself a certificate using crayons, a protractor and the straight side of a butter knife- I couldn't find a ruler. It read in the following way:

Bently Knight no longer exist in this world or any other.
He is now the Lone Ranger.
Forever and ever.
The End.

Ps. This is an official document, just like the one we got down at the courthouse, that day that no one asked me my opinion about any of it.

I asked Mama to frame it too and pretty please, put it on the buffet. But she said-

No.

That's all she said. Just-

No.

Probably just as well as there isn't much room up there anymore anyway since the top of the buffet is where Mama displays her photography. She shoots with a Pinhole camera that she made herself out of an old coffee can. This is how she did it:

Step 1: spray painted the inside of the can and the lid pitch black. The can acts as the box of the camera.

Step 2: took a needle from her sewing kit and poked a hole in the lid. Teeny-tiny!

Step 3: made a shutter out of black electrical tape and aluminum foil. Shutter then taped onto the lid, completely covering the pinhole.

Step 4: placed photo paper on the inside of the can, opposite the hole.

Step 5: put lid back into place on coffee can.

Step 6: this has been how to make a Pinhole camera. Now, you're ready to shoot.

All of the pictures sitting on the buffet have two things in common. The first is that they're all of me at various stages in my life; first day of school, second grade field trip to the zoo, me holding an all A report card-things like that.

The second thing is that since Mama only shoots with a Pinhole, all the pictures look alike to a certain degree. This is because with a Pinhole camera, the center hole where the light enters the box is so tiny that only a small amount is able to pass through it, and only the center of the exposure, where the majority of light hits, is well developed. Conversely, because the rest of the photograph is light deprived, everything else, especially the edges of the film, fades into a mysterious haze, giving the appearance, for example, that I attended my first day of school in a cloud bank.

Mr. Knight says that Mama's pictures look old-timey, like something Butch Cassidy could stumble out of at any time, landing right smack dab in our dining room where he, based upon the reputation of his personality, might be inclined to demand a steak dinner or a back-rub, *Swedish Style*.

"Hrumph," Mama says. "I'd like to see old Butch try."

Mama Ruth says every Sunday that she's taking that piece of furniture back since it was just a loan to begin with, but she never does. I think it's just something she says, not something she means.

Saturday night. I was real excited about watching The Lone Ranger on the re-run channel. Mama said that she thought she'd rather watch Jeopardy since she'd seen all The Lone Rangers about a hundred million times and what time did it come on anyway, Percy? Mr. Knight consulted the guide and it turned out that Jeopardy came on a half-hour after *The Lone Ranger* went off so we would all be okay.

He also said-

Son, your mother and I need to talk to you.

So I said-

Sure thing Mr. Knight, but can it wait? My program just came on!

So then he said-

Sure thing, cowboy. Giddy up!

The three of us sat together on the couch watching the TV Lone Ranger save the day with a little help from his trusty friend Tonto. I shot my gun off two times during the episode, first during a cow rustling scene and then once more when the Ranger shot his up in the air to scare away a pack of buzzards that had commenced to circling above his head. Mr. Knight made the comment that buzzards behaving in that manner could only be interpreted as a bad sign. Mama agreed, then told me to quit shooting that gun in the house Bently, good grief.

After the day was saved, Mr. Knight pressed the off button on the remote control, the image of box of Frosted Flakes making the transition from full to ghost to nothing. The three of us sat there on the couch for a while, Mama and Mr. Knight looking back and forth at each other and practicing their smiles, and me, smelling down the barrel of my gun where the scent from the spent caps still lingered, my nose filling almost to the point of delirium with the delicious smells of the old west. Mama said to quit smelling that gun Bently, it's going to give you some sort of weird brain cancer. I told her yes ma'am, but kept on smelling it anyway. Mama let out a big huffy groan, which apparently was the signal Mr. Knight had been waiting for cause then he started in.

"Bently, your mother and I are concerned about you, son."

I looked over at Mama who seemed to be too consumed with picking cat hair off the arms of the couch to be worried about anything else.

"That true?" I asked her.

She released the fly aways into the air. "Yes sweetheart, it's true," she said, the expression on her face exactly same as the day that she informed me that Ralph was moving on "to a better place." Mr. Knight continued.

"We've made you an appointment with a doctor, a special kind of doctor, a doctor that we think can help you son, can make you feel better."

"But I don't feel bad, Mr. Knight, look here."

To prove my point, I took off from the couch as fast as my chaps would allow, got a running start, then faster than a shoot out in an outhouse, dropped down to my knees and in triumphant glory slid clear across the floor to the far side of the room, where unfortunately, I disturbed a silk plant that Mama had potted in real dirt; a clandestine effort to make it look more authentic. Quick as lightning I jumped to my feet, brushed the soil from my person and spun smoothly around, purposeful *and* intimidating eye contact with both Mama and Mr Knight now becoming my focus. Finally, after a fair amount of staring from both sides, I moved forward towards them by way of a somersault tumble.

"Ta da!" I yelled, sticking the landing like an Olympic gymnast I'd seen on TV. "The Lone Ranger rides again!" *Bang, bang, bang!* In a vigorous display of my good health, I sprayed the air with bullets. *Bang, bang, bang.* Three more times. Well really, I lost count. But, *bang, bang, bang! Bang bang!*

For the big finale, I ran in full circles around the room, all the while expertly spinning my gun on my trigger finger, not once, not twice, but three times! Possibly, I lost count there too, but the important fact to remember here is that I spun that gun in an expert fashion and a whole bunch!

Finally, I holstered my weapon. Because safety first. The demonstration showcasing my radically good health had come to an end.

The display was both exhilarating and exerting and as I stood there breathing out hard from the rush of the moment, trying to catch back up with my breath, Mama started to cry. Mr. Knight pulled her over to him where her face became lost in burial to the enormous girth of his shoulder. They sat like that for a long time, Mama boo-hooing, Mr. Knight consoling.

All of the commotion must have unnerved Whiskers

because she bolted out from under the couch. Frantically she scanned the room for a place to hide, bug-eyed and desperate like a jack rabbit fleeing a fire, her wee-little kitty ears pinned back flat against her head as though she were an unfortunate victim of an invisible tape experiment gone horribly wrong, which I am ashamed to say, did once happen. But only the one time. I learned my lesson. And Mama took away the tape.

"I suggest under the buffet showcasing the certificate, Whiskers!" I yelled after her as she turned the corner vacating the room.

Mama released herself from Mr. Knight's shoulder then wiggled her way out from the depths of the couch onto the edge, her enormous belly leading the way.

"We're going in the morning Bently, down to Little Rock. To see the doctor. He'll be nice, you'll like him. We're leaving early, so let's get you to bed. Give me a hand honey, would you please?"

Mr. Knight stood and pulled her the rest of the way from the couch. On the way up, she blew her nose into a tissue that she routinely kept in her sock when whatever frock she wore lacked the capacity for pockets. A peculiar series of honks and whistles escaped as she waddled in my direction, arm extended, hand reaching; fingers wiggling in the way one charms a cat.

Sensing danger I backed away, just like I would have if one of them old Cavendish boys was after me, then quick as a flash, drew my gun. Naturally, since Mama is a woman and of the weaker sex, I issued a gentlemanly warning.

"Madam, please get back. I do not wish to have to defend myself against a lady."

Her eyes were so puffed up and blood shot red from all the crying that when she squinted them at me, she looked scary as anything I'd ever seen on TV or in real life and I knew by a terrible, gnawing, gut instinct that that thing reaching and grabbing for me right there in my very own living room was no longer my mama, but a terrible monster; a demon had taken hold!

The demon monster moved another step closer to me and when it did, I took a step backward in the opposite direction. Again, the thing moved in closer and I in-turn stepped back, the two of us like competing contestants in a slow moving chasing game. Sensing impending doom of a personal nature, I aimed my gun straight for the beast that once was my mama.

"Bentley, please," the demon spoke in the woman's tongue, "be yourself, just this one time. Let me put you to bed, like you used to let me and stop pointing that gun at me. Percy, do something."

From behind the demon boomed a jagged, crackling voice, the sound like that of a merciless wind as it carves new canyon from a great and mighty mountain.

"I sure will, Lilith."

Then came the beast. A giant of gargantuan proportion, red faced, crazy eyed and worst of all, well appointed in weaponry. Pulling a whip from around its waist, the demon began the exercise of cracking leather across the center palm of an enormous, open claw.

"Bently son, this will hurt me more than it will you, but you give me no choice!"

The giant advanced toward me, whip cracking, earth shaking beneath his feet; the floors of our old house quivering like a feather on the wind. Because I am a man of peace I didn't want to do it, but feeling my life to be in grave danger, I had no choice and so I aimed for the eyes.

Bang, bang bang! Bang bang! Bang! Bang bang bang, bang!

Smoke wrapped itself around me, stinging my eyes, my nose, my throat. There in my cloud of dark the world felt still, safe. I stood fixed, daring not even to breath for fear that any movement might break the sanctuary, waiting for the inevitable thud of the monster going down, which I am sorry to report, never came; alas, the life of a lawman is full of strife. Instead, breaching the temporary safety of my temple came the claw. I am ashamed to admit it but for a second there, I lost my nerve and closed my eyes.

"Damn it, Bently, damn it, son!" The demon raged and grabbed at me, very nearly knocking the hat from my head. He got me by the shoulder and came in close, the vilest of breath shooting directly up my nose. "This stops now!"

I forced myself to open my peepers and when I did, what I saw before me sent quivers up and down the full length of my spine. Pinned to the shroud of the beast was a five-pointed star, menacing and gleaming in gold; the unmistakable sign of the worst kind of evil. This demon, this enormous, terrifying beast from the deep could be none other than Lucifer; the very Devil himself!

And so began the struggle for my life. I knew that there would be no hope if the Devil succeeded in un-arming me so I exercised the only option available; I took my gun and whacked him, hard as I could. *Thwack!* Justice delivered, right up-side the head.

The Devil stumbled backward and landed on the couch, a

course of blood as winding and dirty as the muddy waters of the Rio Grande springing forth from the wound; a liquid stampede of evil!

"Percy, oh, Percy no! Bently, what have you done?" the she-monster cried, rushing to aid the Devil, fast hands flying after the wound.

My feet told me to run, to leave them both behind, and so I did, not even allowing myself one, final look back into that den of iniquity.

Out through the kitchen I flew where clean plates sat drying to the right of the sink and dirty plates sat piled to the left, past the humming icebox where I kept my orange push-up-pops, past the cowering cat named Whiskers.

"Run, Whiskers run!" I yelled. "The devil's in the house!"

The mournful sounds of Lucifer and his concubine followed me out the back door. Hollering, wailing, disappointment, disbelief; a high pitched ball of frantic, collective sorrow.

"You won't get me, you demons!" I yelled back into their lair. "I'm the Lone Ranger. I stand for truth and justice! And the American way!" I threw that last part in for good measure.

Just then Whiskers came running out and so I snatched her up and together we sped out into the coming darkness. "Good girl, Whiskers, good girl," I said, stroking her long mane of silver hair.

I was running so fast that I nearly crashed directly into the tree holding the house that Mr. Knight built me for my birthday, the solar lights spotlighting the ladder just beginning to glow in the early hours of the night.

"Good bye, tree house!" I yelled. "We sure did have some fun!" (Though not as much fun as Mr. Knight would have liked, being that I had yet to agree to the "father-son" sleepover he consistently and annoyingly proposed just about every Friday night of my life; a tedious and exhausting failure on his part, I imagine).

My fellow escapee began to struggle in my arms.

"Now look here, Whiskers, if you wanna go with me you're gonna have to behave."

But I believe her mind was already made up cause no sooner had I given the warning did she break free, running as fast her little legs could carry her back across the yard and into the open door of the demon house.

"Good luck, gal!" I shouted and I meant it. My feelings weren't hurt or nothing, after all, life on the run ain't for everybody. I could hear the demons coming up from behind; the occasion for personal reflection and contemplation had come to an end. I raced for the corn field just beyond the boundary of our yard but when I got there, something was weird. What had been an endless maze of tasseled rows was now transformed into a Wild West canyon measuring at least a million miles long and a thousand miles wide with Prickly Pear and Sage brush dotting the landscape like Poison Ivy bumps on a contaminated arm. I swear that as I stood there taking in the majesty and wonderment of it all, a tumble weed roll right over my foot! Just exactly the kind of place them darned old Cavendish boys would favor. A click, like a television being called into action echoed throughout the canyon, (so loud in fact, that I covered my ears) and that's when things went from weird, on over into the realm of completely amazing! First, this happened:

A red velvet curtain fell from the sky, enclosing the entire canyon.

And this:

The canyon and everything in it, (even me,) faded from color into varying shades of black, white and the deeply toned yellows of the Old West.

Then finally this:

On the bluff above my head a man appeared wearing the distinctive penguin suit of a musical conductor. In his hand he held a baton that when tapped upon the podium produced an orchestra; strings, wood wind, brass, and percussion sections realized one rap at a time.

"Well, I'll be," I said aloud. "I guess I did learn something in music class after all."

The players sat still as Christmas Eve, all eyes fixed on the conductor. Raising the baton up over his head he turned to me. "Lone Ranger, I suggest you whistle," he said with the kind of authority that made me believe I should. Without hesitation I put my fingers to my lips the way Mr. Knight had taught me when Ralph was still around and blew hard as I could and I'll be darned if upon my cue, the whole world didn't explode into sound!

First the came trumpets, then the French horns and trombones. Next up, violins, cellos, flutes and bassoons. Kettle drum, base drum, triangle, snare. And symbols; oh my gosh, symbols! I love symbols! I never get those in class; gol darn rhythm sticks, each and every time.

Da da dum, da da dum, da da dum dum dum. Da da dum, da da dum, da dah dum, dum dum....

Could it be?

Da da dum, da da dum, da dah dum dum dum. DA DAH

DAHHH, DA DAH DA, DAH DAH.....

"The William Tell Overture," the theme song of me; The Lone Ranger! YE HAW!!!!

I fired my pistol into the air, the cacophonous sound of hammer on cap a fine compliment to the glorious celebration already in progress. I twirled till I was dizzy, (falling down more than once,) until perspiration dripped from my forehead onto the star spangled collar of my shirt. But I wasn't the only one. Over at the orchestra cliff the conductor was really working up a sweat. His arms flew to and fro like a scarecrow caught in an all night storm while his head rocked back and forth in time to the furious rhythm of the piece; the movement almost identical to that of a bobble-head doll stationed on the dashboard of a runway Volvo racing through a parking lot. I saw that happen one time, so I would know.

"Whistle again!" he yelled in my direction, his voice fighting mightily to be heard over the exhilarating performance of the orchestra. So once more I pursed my lips and when I did, well good gravy train, you won't believe what happened next!

Up the pass came the great horse, Silver! Mane flying, tail spinning, chest heaving! Feet kicking, body pulsing, legs rearing! Everything I could ever imagine and more. The magnificent creature came to a screeching halt in front of me, then in an effort to express the gentlemanly demeanor of his character, bowed down on one leg, extending the invitation to ride.

"Just in time, boy," I told him, stroking his long golden mane, hair so soft and fine that in the calloused sphere of my hands felt like something more akin to corn silks. I slid my foot into the stirrup and mounted up, then wrapped the reins considerable tight around my hands as preparation for what I knew would be a heck of a ride.

"Giddy up boy, let's go!" I yelled. "Hi-Yo, Silver! Away!"

The great horse's body throbbed, haunches flexing, muscles quivering; a world of horsey brawn housed beneath the saddle and raring to go! Into the air we flew like a bird or a plane or something in between, a combination creature I would draw out later and ask Mama to display in a frame on the buffet beside the adoption.

To the open road! No more bed times, no more nice doctors down in Little Rock. No more demon monsters telling me what to do. The mighty rock cliffs of the canyon would serve as our bedroom walls, the distant howling of a lonely wolf our lullabies. I patted Silver on the neck; we belonged to no one but ourselves.

For miles we traveled over rough terrain and crooked, almost indiscernible trails until we reached the center of the canyon; a deep, hollowed out place where a lazy river flowed under the protection of a twinkling sky, reflections of the stars above us sparkling like diamonds on the surface of the gentle, rippling water. I encouraged Silver to drink and on his back I rested.

"Being the Lone Ranger is hard work, Silver. My thumb hurts from whacking that demon so hard and after riding for such a distance as we have, my rear end is as numb as a polar bear stuck to an iceberg which brings me to a revelation old pal; I never thought about a numb butt as being a possibility. Honestly, I'm a little shocked. The Lone Ranger on TV never says, *Hold up there, Silver, my buttocks sure do need a rest.*

Never. That kind of omission of information tends to leave one unprepared, I suppose. But, I guess that all this traveling is hardest on you since you're carrying the burden of the both of us, so drink up old friend and rest, the road ahead will no doubt prove to be even more treacherous and long."

Silver raised his head from the shimmering pool and turned back to look at me, long, glistening threads of water dripping from his mouth before returning to the stream.

"I'm not tired, Lone Ranger," he said. "I'm a horse, so don't you worry about me. We're down in the valley now, the lowest point of the land. We have but one path to go; the steep and jagged trail up into the mountains. It could be dangerous, Lone Ranger. Some of the other horses from Wild Horse Valley told me them Cavendish boys might be hiding out up there in a mountain shack. Now I don't know about that, but I know we've got to keep on riding. Hold on tight Lone Ranger, no place to go but up!"

He said all that real normal, not at all like Mr. Ed from the re-run channel, none of that head bobbing stuff that you can tell is fake; sugar rubbed strategically between gums to achieve the bogus affect.

Inspired by Silver's fine speech, I tightened my grip on the reins, crossing one stap over the other to form an X the way Mr. Knight had taught me that time he led me round the corral on a fair pony. "That's my boy," he said beaming with pride to a man standing just outside the circle as we made our way around the ring for the first time. "That's not my real Daddy," I said to the same man upon our return. The next time we came back around the man was gone and a stranger stood in his place but this time when we passed by we did so silently, Mr. Knight not even bothering to acknowledge the newcomers existence with a polite nod of his head.

"Hi-Yo, Silver! Away!" I gave the command and like a speeding bullet we were off, the river and its cool refreshment becoming a distant memory. To the upward trail we flew, the echo of Silver's pounding hooves crying as if a warning; the beating of a thousand warrior drums.

"Good one!" returned my faithful companion. "It's my favorite thing when you yell, 'Hi-Yo, Silver! Away!'"

We climbed higher and higher like a moon bound rocket, the Sagebrush and boulders lining the sides of the trail reduced to a series of indiscernible blurs courtesy of my accelerated sight. At one point I mistook a tall, hulking rock formation for Mr. Knight and a disproportionately fat tumbleweed sure did look an awful lot like Mama but I knew those things could not be them, but instead were figments of imagination and speed.

After a few minutes of riding a line of trees came into view, jutting heroically from top of an otherwise scruffy, sparsely vegetated hill.

"Almost there, Lone Ranger," snorted Silver, hot, spent breath hitting the cool night air and rising up like ghost. "Now hold on, cause I'm surging for the top of that peak. Grip with your legs, weight down in the stirrups."

My mind went back to that September day at the fair. "Bet you'd like a pony for yourself one day, Bently," Mr. Knight had asked when my turn with the little horse was done and we were walking over to the Tilt-A-Whirl to get in line. *Of course I want a pony, you dim wit*, I thought but didn't answer aloud knowing better for it. But *now* it didn't matter cause *now* I didn't need an old pony; I had Silver, the horse I had nursed back to good health in episode two. A horse I expected nothing from in return, no loyalty, no companionship, but got it anyway thanks to his grateful animal nature and fine sense of horsey honor.

When we reached the top safe and sound, I patted my mount on the neck. "You did good, Silver." I told him, looking around at all the trees, a forest way more abundant than the view from below had allowed me to foresee. "Looks like we made it to the safety of the deep woods. Nobody will find us here and now we can put our heads together and figure out what to do about them Cavendish boys."

Silver snorted, pawed at the ground. "Lone Ranger," he said, "someone waits for you."

I squinted my eyes in the darkness, the moon now engulfed in a passing cloud. "Where, Silver? I don't see nobody."

"There," said the horse, his hoof raised and pointing. "By that crooked tree."

Just then the moon sprang free from the cloud, soft, glowing light returning to the earth and illuminating the figure of a man. I reckon he was no more than fifteen, twenty feet in front of us, hunched over close to the ground in what looked to be a mighty uncomfortable position. I cued Silver forward and as we approached the mysterious stranger looked up and smiled. "Kemosahbee," he said, "me have found path."

"Do I know you?" I called out, bringing my eyes to full squinch for a better look.

"Kemosahbee, it me."

We stood directly in front of him now, the prime location enabling me to get a good look. After a seconds worth of careful examination I knew who it must be, but somehow he didn't look quite right. Where was the buckskin suit? Where was the fringe? Where were the moccasins, for gosh sakes? On the plus side, his hair *was* done up in a braid, the length of it falling down the middle of his back and he did look at least part Indian, but that's where the similarities ended.

"Tonto, that you?" I asked.

"You betcha it me, for sure."

"Well, where's your suit?"

He shrugged his shoulders up and down. "At cleaners. Wear this instead," he said standing up and pulling his tie-dyed t-shirt out in front of him so that I could make out the words printed across the front; *Parrothead Nation, trespassers will be offered a shot.*

"Hmmmm okay, but what's that you're wearing on your bottom, looks like surf shorts."

"Swim trunk, Kemosahbee, built in drawers. Keep package tight."

"Well, where's Scout?" I asked looking around for his horse.

"Upgraded to golf cart. Better horse power. See, look there." He pointed a couple feet away to a clearing in the brush where a brand spanking new golf cart sat, its only blemish a bumper sticker spread at a lazy angle across the front; *It's five o'clock somewhere!* I couldn't believe what I was hearing. Or seeing.

"A golf cart! What did you do with her? Seriously, where is Scout?"

"She at farm. Same farm as Ralph. Ralph say 'hi,' by the way."

"He did? Well, I'll be." Knowing that the two of them were together made me feel a little better. "Okay, I guess that's okay," I said, I think mainly in an attempt to comfort myself. "Can't spend all night worrying on it anyway, can we? We've got to catch them Cavendish boys. Silver heard they might be holed up in a mountain cabin somewhere around these parts. But before I forget, what's going on with that tree, Tonto? Why's it bent over and pointing that-a-way?" I asked, nodding in the direction of the tree.

"Kemosahbee, my people took sapling trees, bent trunks in certain direction. Trees grew, made path; show which way we go. It map, Kemosahbee. We follow map to Cavendish. Follow bent trees, Kemosahbee, you, me. Let bent trees lead us. To justice. To truth."

I considered his speech, especially the part about the path leading us to them darned old Cavendish boys and how justice could finally be served and I while that sounded real good, I had a few questions to ask before we headed off in hot pursuit.

"Tonto, where have you been?"

"What you mean, Kemosahbee?"

"Well," I said, wiggling around in the saddle, my rear in desperate need of a more comfortable spot. "I sure could have used your help back there at the house. Something terrible happened. Mama and Mr. Knight done turned into demons and practically tried to eat me for dinner! And, before that, they did kissing right in the middle of my show, directly there beside me on the couch while I was trying to watch and before that, I got adopted!"

"Hmm, Kemosahbee, that bad."

"You bet it is, Tonto, it's really bad and that's not all. They want me to go see a doctor down in Little Rock," I said, cuing

Silver onto the path as directed by the bent over tree.

"You sick, Kemosahbee?" Tonto asked, taking a key fob from his pocket and giving it a click, the golf cart springing to life and giving a little, "toot!"

"Naw, ain't nothing wrong with me and anyway, its not that kind of doctor. It's a talking doctor."

"Talking doctor, Kemosahbee?" he asked, mounting up and revving the engine a couple of times before putting it into drive, then falling in-line beside Silver and me.

"Yea, it's for my head."

"Your head hurt, Kemosahbee?"

I thought about the question for a minute before I answered, the sound of Silver's clip-clopping and the low hum of the golf cart engine filling the silence.

"Well, yes and no, Tonto," I finally said. "It's not like the kind of head hurts that Mama gets forcing her have to take a lie down. That's a headache. With me, it's more like what I'm thinking about hurts cause there's just too much of it in my brain and my head can't hold it all and it spills to the outside. I swear Tonto, there's enough stuff in my head for two people. In fact, sometimes I feel like I've got two completely different people stuck in there!"

"Two people in one head, Kemosahbee? That one too many."

"Yea, that's what Mama says, or that's what she used to say before she let Mr. Knight do all her talking for her. And anyway, she's the one that needs a doctor. She's all swell up, looks like she swallowed a watermelon."

"A watermelon, Kemosahbee?"

"Yep, a watermelon, and a big one; whole. She's tired all the time too, seems like every time I see her she's falling asleep in a chair or has her head down on the table. Sometimes even, Mr. Knight makes my dinner because Mama's so tired she can't do it."

"What he make you?"

"Mainly hot dogs."

"Hmmm, Kemosahbee. Hot dogs about fifty-fifty in my book."

"Yea, I know it. Hot dogs are all right some of the time, but not all of the time. One night he did make tuna fish, but it tasted funny so I gave it to Whiskers. She wouldn't even eat it!"

"Wowzers, Kemosahbee. That real bad!"

"Yea," I agreed, but didn't expand on it cause already I'd thought of something else that seemed more pressing. "You know, I think maybe she's just fat."

"Whiskers, Kemosahbee?"

"Naw Tonto, Mama. I think she's fat and that's why she's tired all the time. That's gotta be a lot of work, carrying around all that extra weight. At least that's what Mama Ruth tells her. And anyway, what else could it be?"

"Hmmmmm," said Tonto, obviously thinking about what else it could be.

"Hmmmmm," said me, obliviously not.

"Tonto," I said, glancing over at the cart.

"Yes, Kemosahbee."

"Your lights aren't on."

"Whoops! Me do that all time," he laughed, leaning down and and punching them on, the trail before us now swaddled in a crisp, artificial light. My mind returned to the solar lights marking the ladder leading up into the tree house. Had they too been pressed into full service at the request of their own battery; a slender, black devise whose sole responsibility lie in gathering warmth from the sun before sending it out by installments to each bulb, like the gradual revelations of a cereal TV show.

We rode on for a while, the trail taking us higher and higher into the mountains, Silver tackling the treacherous terrain with the sure-hoofedness of a well seasoned war horse. The golf cart held it's own too, the 110 horse power engine cycling through one steady series of rotations after another as Tonto thumbed through the driver's manual, at times reading aloud information that he considered to be of mutual interest.

"Climb to the highest heights with The Urban Snake Charmer 5000, and, *With the largest rechargeable battery on the market, you'll harness the power of nature with the world's first eight volt rechargeable solar battery: Your independence is a gift from the sun!"*

"That's real nice, Tonto," I might say after each shared passage, and, "We'll, that sure is interesting." Pleasantries like that.

Off in the distance I heard a hoot owl call out, and a coyote send out a question in the form of a long, lonely howl; the response abbreviated and terse, as if the next coyote down the chain didn't have the time to thoroughly explain. Crickets sang, Katydids hummed and I was so lost in the trance of it all that I almost didn't notice the next tree bent and drafted into service.

"Look, Tonto, another directional tree!" I called out in much jubilation.

I cued Silver to a canter and Tonto stepped on the gas. In

no time flat we'd dismounted, my faithful Indian companion reaching the tree first and with gentle fingers exploring the manipulated trunk of the bowing, ancient Spruce.

"This good sign, Kemosahbee," he said, flipping a branch over to examine the other side. "Trail keep going up. We on right path, Kemosahbee."

"Alright, let's keep going, if you think that we should.

"Why we not go, Kemosahbee?"

"Well, for one thing," I answered, looking straight ahead. "*That* tree points directly into the mouth of *that* cave. I don't know about that." Except that I did and didn't want to go. With the exception of reading time under the blankets, small, dark places had never appealed to me much.

"You be fine, Kemosahbee," Tonto said, waving his hand in front of his face as if dismissing my fears by symbolically wiping them away. I did not feel encouraged.

"Yea, well maybe, but for starters, how we even gonna get through that teeny-tiny opening. I *maybe* could squeeze through, but I doubt if you can. Ain't no way Silver and the golf cart are going through there."

"Lone Ranger, you go first. We follow. It work fine. Tonto promise."

"What do *you* think, Silver," I asked hoping for an opinion closer to that of my own, but when he didn't answer, I looked around to see why not and why not was this: Silver, the greatest stallion ever to place a hoof on the desert sands of the Old West was off in the bushes, coughing up a hair ball. "Silver, good golly! I called. What you doin' that for?"

He backed up a few feet to free himself from the brush, then licked his arm and brought it up over his head, stroking himself like a cat. "Don't mind me, Lone Ranger," he said going over his ears, "just taking care of business."

"Holy smokes," I said, looking back at Tonto. "Now what?"

"Now, we go, Kemosahbee."

"Oh, alright," I said, but what I didn't say but wanted to was, *I'll go, but I won't like it.*

I called Silver and mounted up then took off for the cave with Tonto and the golf cart following closely behind.

"I still don't see how we're going to fit through there," I said, as the three of us plus the golf cart stood hovering just in front of the opening, a hole of staggeringly small proportions.

"Close eyes, Kemosahbee," Tonto instructed. "Just go."

I'll go, but I won't like it." There. I said it-couldn't help it, but at the same time, I did close my eyes. "And by the way, Silver, a hair ball is beneath your dignity." I couldn't help but say that too, a statement to which the horse did not respond.

If I hadn't been there myself, I would have never believed it possible but wonders upon wonders, we made it through, though beyond the miracle of our unlikely entry in the cave, there were no more surprises. The place was cold and dark, and depressing as heck. If it hadn't been for the headlights of *The Urban Snake Charmer 5000*, I wouldn't have been able to make my hand out right in front of my own eyes and for the first time since we'd started out, I found myself understanding Tonto's decision to retire Scout, but I still didn't like it.

"Shew-ee, Lone Ranger!" Silver complained, plugging his nose with a hoof. "This place stinks big time."

He was right. The whole place smelled damp and mildewy, closed in like a house locked up for a long time, suddenly opened and in desperate need of airing. But worse than the cold or the dark or even the stench of the place was the feeling it gave me. Plain as day, I could feel the heebie jeebies creeping up my spine only to Custer's Last Stand squarely on the back of my neck and digging right in, just exactly like the time Mama woke me up screaming from her place beside me on the bed. Mama Ruth says that feeling comes when somebody's walking over your grave, a scenario making the situation even worse.

"What is this place, Tonto?" I asked, keeping my voice to a whisper, intuition telling me I should. "It's creepy."

"Ah, Kemosahbee, my people call this place 'The Insides'. " His voice was normal, calm even, like he wasn't spooked at all; like he was used to the damp, at home in the dark.

"You not scared, Tonto?"

"No, Kemosahbee. Me been here before. Many times."

I guess I should have felt some comfort knowing that he'd survived this place which so unnerved me, but I didn't. The further on we traveled into the cave, the more heebie jeebies I got racing up and down my spine, more traffic over my grave. And I started missing Mama real bad, I think more than I ever had; more than when she had to stay at the hospital even after I was discharged and sent home with Mama Ruth.

Memory of the fight back home washed over me like a wave, and all at once I felt to be drowning in regret. I ached with a new kind of sadness and I couldn't help but wonder; had there been a way to avoid that latest confrontation or was it bound to happen sooner or later, Mama and Mr. Knight teaming up and joining forces against me, nobody taking my side but me?

Eventually the path through the cave narrowed down to a

single file only situation, forcing Tonto to slow the cart and take his place in line behind Silver and me. "Follow the leader," he sang merrily, as if we were out for a spring-time romp. *The Insides.* Worse than a cracked closet door at midnight on Halloween night.

Up in the lead I became acutely aware of my solitude, a burden revealing itself in stages throughout the many vulnerable places of my body. I felt the loneliness first in my throat; I couldn't swallow right. Next my eyes; heavy tears welling up with no place to go but out. But worst of all I felt the heartache in my chest, shooting pains like stabbing knives working their way around until my insides felt turned out. A panic attack, and Mr. Knight was nowhere near to talk me through it.

Concentrate on your breathing, that's all you gotta do. You can do this, you've got it, son.

But when I did, things quickly turned disastrous with the opposite effect taking hold, rendering me unable to breath at all. I turned back to Tonto for help.

"Tonto, help me! I can't breath!" I shouted, but it was no use; he was asleep at the wheel. For about half a second I wondered if I should worry about that, but decided that under the current circumstances, dying of asphyxiation was most likely a more pressing development than that of a dozing Indian sleep-driving at the helm of a golf cart.

Thinking maybe we could go out the same way we came in, I cued Silver to turn around, a command he flatly ignored. Even if he hadn't though, it probably wouldn't have mattered as the trail was too narrow to turn back.

The Insides. If I had any doubt before, I didn't now; I was going to die. Watch out Saint Peter cause here I come!

But then like a lightning bolt to the head, Mr. Knight's voice crashed into my brain.

Let's play the game, son, let's play the game.

The rules to the game are simple: if I can manage to take a breath in, I can say anything in the whole entire world that I want without fear of reprisals, even if it makes someone mad or sad; even if it's a curse word! Same thing with a breath out, but only if Mama isn't around. The game is Mr. Knight's idea, not hers and honestly, I don't think she has any idea of its existence.

I started off small, with a deep breath in: "Mama." Then a deep breath out: "Adoption."

Deep breath in: "Mr. Knight." Deep breath out: "Ain't my *real* daddy."

I guess from there the whole thing took on a predictable slant; me reading from the script I keep locked up in my head. I really do try to think of other things, honest injun, but other things just won't come.

Deep breath in: "My *real* daddy," deep breath out, "where the hell is he?" That one hurt-not enough air yet. Mama Ruth said the last time she heard anything from him he was down in Florida living near the beach with some woman and her kids in a trailer park. "Five kids," she reported, as if she were reading the evening news, a look of disgust crawling all over her face. "I bet you money not a one of them shares the same patriarchal DNA."

From there my brain went directly to the time them darned old Cavendish boys broke in the house.

Deep breath in: "They hurt Mama," deep breath out, "real

bad."

If my real Daddy had a stuck around, he would have been there to help me fight off those cowards; sons-a-bitches. They never would have held that knife to my throat, digging the tip of the blade in just enough to stop Mama from fightin'.

Look away, Bently—don't look at Mama. Look at the wall, baby. Please, Bently, look away from Mama.

Deep breath in: "If it hadn't been for that," deep breath out, "she never would a met Mr. Knight." In my imagination, I've destroyed the radio sounding out the call a thousand times over; a constant box of static mounted on the dashboard of his patrol car.

Afterwards, I sat on Mama Ruth's lap at the hospital sucking on a butterscotch candy while the doctor looked in my ear, the tip of the Otoscope tickling me something fierce. "Hold steady there, young man," he said, "just making sure you've got everything in there you need."

Mama Ruth wrapped her arms around my middle. "I used to play out there in those woods when I was a girl," she said, motioning toward the window with her head. "Just about your age, Bently." I looked out through the glass to see a forest uncloaked by winter; naked limbs purged of decoration, poised and waiting for springtime's green.

"I did too," said the doctor, now moving the instrument on over to my nose. "I built my first secret club house out there, Tee-Pee style. Made it out of fallen branches, mainly Oak and Pine. Boys only, of course."

"Of course," Mama Ruth said, nodding and smiling. For a moment the doctor paused, the movement of the scope coming to an uncomfortable conclusion while still plugged into the cavity of my nose. Now he joined her in staring out the window, the two of them straining to see beyond the skeleton work of the trees. "I never tore it down," he confessed, a far away look in his eye. "I just got too old for it and quit going out there. I wonder if it might still be there."

"Best not to wonder," Mama Ruth counseled. "You can't ever go back."

"I suppose not," he agreed, retracting the scope and not a moment too soon I might add, the placid, dreamy look in his eyes now gone. "Open wide there, young man," he said, taking a popsicle stick from his pocket and shoving it into my mouth. "Let's see what's going on down the old cake shoot."

The breathing was coming easier now but based on past experience, I knew better than to retire from the game just yet so on I went, my thinking coming back around to Mama.

Deep breath in: "She said I was just a child, a helpless baby child." Deep breath out: "That it wasn't my job to take care of her, that we needed a *real* man around the house." Enter, Mr. Percival Octavius Knight.

They made me carry the ring at the wedding, a twinkling circle of diamonds and polished gold. *What a perfect little gentleman*, all the old ladies cooed in an eerie, unrehearsed unison as I walked down the aisle. All except for Mama Ruth who sat silent and still as a statue as if she were attempting to blend in with the intricate engravings dressing the end of the pew, an enormous white lily pinned to her dress in the spot where the missing breast had once been. The wedding was a turning point; not long after that the adoption happened.

"Bently son, I sure am glad I found you and your mama," Mr. Knight told me one day over an ice cream at the drive-in.

"My whole life, all I ever wanted was to be a husband and a daddy. True, circumstances were not ideal when we met, but The Lord works in mysterious ways."

"He sure does," I agreed, looking up at the sky and flashing my angriest face at Heaven. "Thanks for nothing, God," I mumbled into my cone.

Silver slowed to halt. "What is it, boy?" I asked, looking around. "Do you see something?"

"Fraid so, Lone Ranger," he said, stomping a hoof, "and my horse sense is telling me to be wary."

"Wary of what?" I asked, anticipating impending doom and so sinking down a good six inches into the saddle.

"Of that," Silver said, his ears pointing forward.

I can describe it in no other way but as a man wrapped in a cloud. Slowly, he moved through the darkness, the glow from a lantern held in a puffy, cartoonishly built hand illuminating his face-the only human looking part of his body-the fickle wick of the flame splashing shadows like rain drops across the uneven surface of his skin.

"Silver, back up. We've gotta get out of here," I whispered.

"No can do, Lone Ranger. Too narrow and besides...." He never got to finish.

"Toll, please," the cloud man said waving the beacon side to side, beams of light swaying to and fro as if illuminating a swinging trapeze.

"Toll?" I managed to ask.

He moved closer in, the lantern and its shifting light a mesmerizing tool, like that of a hypnotist's jewel.

"Toll there, young un. You do know what a toll is, don't you, feller?"

"No sir, I don't."

"What's that you say?"

"I say, I don't know what a toll is, sir."

"Huh, well, that's an easy one. Some things are hard, but describing what a toll is ain't one of them. Now let me think for just a minute and I'll describe it to you, the best way that I can." His mouth worked its way through a series of mumbling but I could make out no discernible words. After a minute he stuck a finger straight up in the air. "Got it," he said, then started in on the explanation.

"Sonny, there are any number of definitions I could use in describing the meaning of the word *toll*, but for the purposes of this conversation, I'll focus my explanation on just one. Here we go," he said, dangling his free hand in front of my face and turning it palm side up. "That'll be a dollar."

I was so confused and frustrated that I almost bit my lip in half. "Mr," I said, "What in the Sam Hill are you talkin' about?"

"A dollar, Mr. Skip. You pay me one dollar, and I let you pass around me over to the exit and on out of this cave. Now, hand it over, I know you got it."

Confused and frustrated disappeared, now I was just plain scared. I looked around for reinforcements but both Tonto and the Urban Snake Charmer were gone! I turned back to the cloud man. "What did you do with Tonto, you son of a bitch cloud man!"

"There, there simmer down dwarf kicks, I've done nothing with em'. Tonto paid his toll long ago. He's already on the outside."

"That's impossible!" I screamed. "He never passed me this

whole time, he couldn't have, the trail's too narrow. You're a liar!"

A queer look came across the cloud mans face, his eyes softened and grew wet, like a puddle gathering rain. "Look here, I don't appreciate your insinuations. I am many a thing, but a liar ain't one of them. He didn't pass you, he just took a side exit out, same as always."

"Yea? I didn't see a side exit. If there had been one, I should would had taken it."

"Oh really, you would have? Now who's the liar. There are side exits all over this place but you never thought to look for one, so focused on that mess in your head you can't see straight or sideways or even upside down. You're missing it all, Lone Ranger; missing, it, all."

I slumped down further into the saddle and dropped the reins, somehow instinctively knowing that the time had come for me to dismount. I slid down off Silver and took a few steps toward the toll keeper.

"I don't have a dollar," I said turning out my pockets for the proof, my hands shaking like leaves caught in the moment of being blown from the tree. "What'da I have to do get out of here, Mister?"

"Well, as it just so happens, there is a back up plan for exiting. You'd be surprised at how many children come through here unprepared to pay the toll. Alls you gotta do is step over there into that photo booth situated directly behind me and get your picture taken. After you smile for the camera, the back of the booth opens and you slide right out of the mountain. Easy as Rhubarb pie. Got it?"

I leaned around to get a look and sure enough, right behind

the cloud man stood a tightly built rectangular building, the exterior plastered and shining with the same plastic glow-in-the-dark stars Mr. Knight had applied to my bedroom ceiling-an attempt to calm my fear of the dark after Mama moved out of my room and into theirs. Seemed easy enough, maybe too easy. I was suspicious.

"Sounds too easy, Mister. What's the catch?"

"No catch there, memory card, but in order to get the back door to open, you have to wait for your picture to develop, then look at it good before you paste it on the wall in the booth."

"I can't take it with me?" I asked

"Now, what would be the point in that? No, leave it on the wall like your spossed to. Now get on in there, I'll take care of your horse."

I looked back over my shoulder at Silver. There on the ground lay history's greatest horse companion, curled tightly into a ball and snoring; not a care in the world. "He'll be alright?" I asked, making my way over to the booth.

"Right as rain," the cloud man laughed, flashes of lightning passing in waves over the surface of his body and like an X-ray, illuminating what looked to be nothing more than a child's drawing of stick figure hiding beneath the cloudy exterior; thunder like God rolling potatoes over the cellar floor narrating the display. "Storms a coming," he said, following closely behind, the lantern now steadied and lighting the path to the booth, like the spotlight does as a courtesy for the lead actor in a play.

"Now remember, short stack, it's easy," he said, opening the door. "Step one: take the picture. Step two: stick it on the wall.

Step three: exit out the back door. Step four: never come back."

"Oh, you don't have to worry one bit about that last one," I said, stepping into the box. "I'm never coming..." The door slammed behind me. "...back."

The word *panic* couldn't even begin to describe it. Pitch black terror, maybe? Nah, that's not even close. The place was utterly and completely void of light. Tingles splayed wide across the back of my neck and down through my arms, my stomach dropping into the black water hole of itself. Sweet Baby Ruth, what had I gotten myself into this time?

"Hey, mister," I yelled, my fist rolled into a ball and banging on the door, "it's dark in here! Where's the light?" Dead silence from the cloud man's side of the wall, but from mine, blood curdling, hair standing up on the back of your neck, wish you could just die already shrieking. Only it wasn't me doing it; I wasn't alone.

I can't describe the desperation, the unmitigated fear, me standing in the tar hill dark not knowing what kind of beast lurked there in the corners; what it might do to me. I reached to all sides, frantic fingers fumbling for the hard plastic of a light switch. "Who's there?" I demanded. "Show yourself right now!" After a minute of finding no such light inducing apparatus, I gave up and drew my gun.

"Show yourself, you coward!" I commanded turning a full circle, shots flying in every direction. *Bang, Bang, Bang!* "Don't you know who I am?"

Suddenly, the screaming stopped. "Oh, I know who you are," came a voice, hastily reconfigured from shrieking to conversational, "but do you?"

Before I could say, *of course I know who I am, you disturber of the peace,* a single, naked bulb crackled to life above my head, the sound almost exactly like that of a hammer breaking the driver's side window of a sheriff's patrol car, which both Mama and Mr. Knight made me promise I would never do ever again as long as I lived. I took a step back and shielded my eyes, so long had I been in the dark that this new found brightness overwhelmed my still somewhat muzzled senses. *Well no wonder;* I thought, looking around the place. I couldn't believe it. I was standing in a hall of mirrors!

"Where are you?" I asked, searching through the resplendent space. "I don't see you."

"No?" the voice teased. "Take your picture, maybe that will clear things up."

I remembered the cloud man's instructions: *take your picture, paste it on the wall, go out the back door, never come back.* I was more than willing, but when I looked for a camera to face or a button to press I could find neither one, the search instead yielding only brilliant manipulations of me-fat me, short me, super skinny tall me, trigger happy me.

"How's it work?" I asked the voice.

"Oh, that's easy. Face any wall and say, *ready.*"

"Should I smile?"

"Up to you, no hard or fast rules in this place, except for the hard and fast rules of course, and if you don't follow those, you never get out. Of course."

Never get out? No thank you; I was gettin' out. I picked a wall at random and turned to face it, just happened to be super skinny tall wall, but no matter. I holstered my gun, tucked in the corners of my shirt, puffed out my chest and smiled. "Ready," I said, through what appeared reflected on the mirrored wall as ridiculously exaggerated teeth. The light above my head flickered like a flash bulb does on a camera as instantaneously, a photograph appeared in my hand, the weight of it startling me in the same way that finding a black snake on my pillow would; not life-threatening or anything, but still, unexpected and unnerving. I brought the picture to my face, studied it, turned it over, shook it out the way I'd seen Mama do her negatives in the walk-in-closet darkroom, but something was wrong.

"Excuse me," I said to the voice, "but this ain't me."

"Isn't you? Whatever do you mean?"

"Well, for starters, it's a picture of a Christmas tree. True, it's a little crooked and bent over, but a Christmas tree all the same. "

"A Christmas tree? How terribly odd. Are you sure?"

"Pretty sure. It's a tree and its got ornaments hanging all over it. Matter of fact, I'm no where to be seen in this picture."

"Why don't you look again, Lone Ranger, just to make absolutely sure that the photograph you hold in your hand does in fact only show the likeness of a Christmas tree and that you are in no way, shape or form featured in that picture one bit, whatsoever, so help you God, you do so solemnly swear."

"Well alright, but I'm telling you, it ain't me," I said flipping the image back over to the front and bringing it right up to my face. "That there is definitely a Christmas tree, I can tell because it's decorated and a Christmas tree is the only kind of tree you adorn. There's a bell....no wait, it's not a bell, it's a .....it's the top of baby bottle."

"Most peculiar. What would *that* be doing hanging on a Christmas tree?"

"Hold on, it's, not that, it's a..... Ah!," I screamed, dropping the picture to floor. I fell back against the wall, panting the way Mama used to do after she'd chased Ralph around the yard demanding he, *drop it right now, Ralph!* "Why," I asked the voice, "is Mama Ruth's cut-off Cancer breast hanging on a tree?"

"We'll get to that in a minute, but first tell me, what else do you see in the picture?"

"Do I have to?" I asked.

"Indeed you do, if you want to get out of this photo booth, you certainly do."

I stooped down to retrieve the photo. "I was wrong," I conceded, sitting down on the floor and staring at the tree. "It's not a Christmas tree."

"Really? Then what is it?"

"It's a nightmare tree."

There it was, every worry, every anxiety, every fear I had ever known or imagined put into form and hanging like family treasures on the branches of a lopsided tree; the framed adoption certificate, a wedding photo of Mama and Mr. Knight, an enormous, distended belly.

My cowboy and Indian sheets peeled from the bed right after the attack, bloodied and wadded onto the floor, bright yellow police tape marking the emergency.

Ralph, his body broken and manipulated into the shape of a question mark and finally a Tonto-esque type figure, his face obscured by sunglasses, a beer in his hand, toes dug into the sand.

"We are the sum of our parts, Lone Ranger. Do you understand?" the voice asked, softly, gently.

"Yea," I answered quietly, my head hung between my knees, hot tears falling from my eyes and landing squarely onto the picture, its glossy finish dissolving under the influence of my sadness; the grisly images streaking and bleeding out into a chemically tinted blur.

"Only one way to get out of a nightmare, Lone Ranger."

"How?" I whispered.

"By waking up."

I heard a release. Then there was nothing, just silence. The voice was gone.

I don't know how long I sat on the floor of that booth staring at what remained of the picture, for the first time seeing what I had become or how long it took for me to decide that enough was enough but finally I knew; being the sum of too many painful parts was getting me no where. And I was tired, so dog-dead tired of being brave all the time. Nobody should have to be brave all the time, not even The Lone Ranger.

I wish I could say that it was easy, simple, instantaneous, painless even but I can't because it wasn't; the whole process was miserable, tedious and slow. Each time I thought of Mama on that bed, those men taking turns writhing back and forth across her body, the way she cried, the way they laughed and moaned, I blubbered so hard that I got the worst case of hiccups this side of the Rio Grande, the end result being that, for lack of a better solution, I was forced to puke in my hat.

"I guess I'm done with that," I said as carefully, I placed it up-right in the corner of the booth.

When I thought of Mr. Knight slipping that ring on Mama's finger I bloodied my hands punching the walls, the skin covering my knuckles splitting upon impact with the mirrors, fine lines and fissures spreading across the shining surface like the splintered shell of a fallen egg.

For the loss of Mama Ruth's breast, I pulled out a clump of my own hair and stomped it until it no longer looked like the thing that it was. If I'd had Papa Jim's lighter, I would have set it afire and danced round it, watching it burn.

In the mourning of Ralph, I whistled until my lips refused to repeat the puckered shape. "There's no Farm!" I yelled, to no one but me. "Farm, my sore ass!"

By the time I got around to studying the delicate nuances surrounding the circumstances of my real daddy leaving, there was nothing left to puke in, punch or pull out. Heck, I'd even run out of hateful words to shout. Truth be told, what was there to really think about? He was gone and wasn't coming back; no amount of introspective soul searching or exploratory debate was going to change that. I had to let him go and with him the mystery of why he didn't love me and Mama enough to stay. Somethings you just never know. That's life for you, I guess. Still though, it stinks. Big time.

So, when it came time to yell my final *ready* up at the ceiling, I truly was ready, my portrait revealing it as truth. I pasted the picture to the wall just like I was supposed to and as I did the back door of the booth opened up just like it was supposed to and I walked out that booth a free man. I didn't feel angry with Mr. Knight or with Mama anymore. I wasn't scared for Mama Ruth. I was looking forward to being a big brother, and not to a watermelon either, but to my baby brother that based on the size of Mama's belly, would be coming any day. *God please*, I prayed in my head, *just don't let it be a girl*. I know that when it comes to sexing a baby the odds are fifty-fifty, but still,

I felt praying for a brother was worth a shot.

I ran across the backyard to my tree house and climbed on up the ladder where once inside I found Whiskers asleep in a pile of cornstalks and scattered silks. I scooped her into my arms and sat with my back against the wall, stroking her chin and watching the sun rise, each second of that great star's ascension bringing with it the sparkling color of a new day; twinkling blues and lilac pinks-saturated hues chasing away the mottled grays and tempered yellows of the old west.

A breeze makes its way in one window and out the other, on its way through gently rustling the corners of a picture tacked to the wall. It's a photograph Mama took on my last birthday showing me and Mr. Knight standing in front of the just completed tree house. There's a big bow wrapped around the trunk of the tree and the grin on my face spans ear to ear-just like that of Mr. Knight's. He stands right behind me, his hands firmly but tenderly pressing down into the meat of my shoulders and when I look at them now in the picture I can almost feel their touch. Mama is in the picture too, but just her thumb. In a rare bit of incompetence on her part, the digit sticks up as if signaling approval, though fuzzy and slightly out of focus. Honestly, that thumb looks like a glowing banana. When I can get my hands on a pen, I think I'll draw a face on it.

I hear someone yell my name, *Bently*, and I shout that I am here, here in the tree.

The Mermaid Tale

I first became acquainted with the five stages of loss the time Daddy threw me into the lake and drowned me. With the luxury of retrospect, I now know that preemptively, I was mourning my own death. But at the time, as I struggled to stay afloat the chilly waters of Lake Morone, all I could think of was, *Surely my own daddy won't let me drown.* That folks, is a textbook case of *Denial,* coming in first on my personal list followed closely by.....

Isolation: I got to know this feeling when Daddy, using the flat end of the paddle, pushed my struggling self as far away from the boat as his arms could reach.

"You're on your own, kid. Better swim it up!" he yelled, taking a bottle of Budweiser from the cooler. "No, not like that," he instructed through the side of his mouth, the bottle now plugged-in and rearranging the even plain of his lips.

"Think light, be breezy; *relax*. You'll swim easy peasy, just like a mermaid."

I think, had I possessed the facilities to do so, I would have rolled my eyes at this fluff; information revealing itself to be virtually useless, like knowing only half of an algorithm or possessing the ability to recall the exact number of concave craters pocking the surface of the moon, like acne scars.

"Please, Daddy, I'll clean my...." I yelled back at what now appeared to be a frozen image rising above my head; my father, the amber bottle at his lips, indulging in a long, ethereal swill, as if he didn't have one care in the whole wide world.

But I, a person whose flailing arms and sputtering mouth suggested closer kinship to an outboard motor than to that of the floating man above, was not having a very good day. *We want air*, my brain kept reminding me, *air, and to finish our sentence, to say the word, room*. Like it would have mattered. I had nothing with which to barter and Daddy knew it; I kept my room tidy as a pin, that morning was no exception. *Bargaining*. Big. Fat. Failure.

Then *Depression*, because let me tell you, when you understand that truly, you have about as good a shot at floating as a cinder block and that honest to Pete, you're going to die during a swimming lesson, it is seriously the most depressing thing you can encounter. I think it must be a good deal ironic too, but as I was only eleven when I died, I don't have that one on great authority, but still, I strongly suspect.

Finally, after what seemed like a lifetime of doing battle with a muddy lake, (lake always wins-home field advantage) I came to *Acceptance*.

This goober is really going to let me die. What a jerk. I quit flapping my arms, let go of my breath. I don't know why, but I very distinctly remember the odd sense of relief I felt when for the first time, water encroached upon the top curvature of my ear. Maybe because I knew that at the very least, I would be saved from hearing anymore of Daddy's nonsensical suggestions, even if from nothing else.

I should point out that this was my first and formal introduction to swimming. It's how *my* daddy's, daddy taught him to swim and his daddy's, daddy taught him and so on and so forth before him.

"Just throw the kid in the water," the fore-daddies said. "They'll either learn to swim or die trying-up to them." And while my daddy and his daddy and so on and so forth all chose to live, by the time I got to the point of *Acceptance*, I was too worn out to try any more and so I chose to die.

It was the first decision I had ever made on my own in my whole entire life. Mama still picked out my clothes each day before school and every night when dinner rolled around she would say, "Try it, you'll like it," and so I did and she was right; I *did* like it. Mama, being a rule follower herself, never strayed from a recipe and consequently, was a really good cook. Everything she made tasted good, even things that shouldn't have, anomalies such as Boiled Squash and Parsnip Stew or Sardine Salad. Beef Stroganoff was always her specialty, a dish generously served with a full helping of cartoon-ish, Swedish accent as the side: *Would-a-you like-a-the stroganoffa-nowa deaha?*

At the playground, Daddy picked out what piece of equipment we would play on, always and never varying from the swings, and I, like the peaceable child I was trained to be, would simply shrug my shoulders and nod my head, the words, "Alright, Daddy," escaping my stupid, smiling mouth even as the linguistic center of my mind would fervently chant, see-saw, see-saw.

Nana Cotton sat with me after school while Mama and Daddy worked and even she made all my decisions for me; like what I would eat for my snack, (Fiber Nice Prunes) when we would work my homework together, (four o'clock exactly) and which neighborhood child could come over and play with me and which one couldn't, (always Naomi Peterson, the preacher's kid but never Bethany Sparks, the amateur tattoo artist).

I never gave so much as a whimper in protest when my plate was too full, nary a rolled eye or condescending snort over those miserable prunes; never once did I run past my daddy in a coup like attempt for the see-saw.

Up until the day I died, my life had been one big automatic shoulder shrugging and okay festival, starring me as my spineless self, obediently performing my best trick center ring; never, ever, ever, putting up any kind of fuss. And all this because I was Mama and Daddy's only child due to the fact that Mama had a list of miscarriages a mile long.

From the very beginning of my miraculous life, I had been instructed to never argue, never have any of my own contrary ideas, never put my foot down about anything; to just go along. Don't make any trouble because trouble makes stress and stress make unborn babies die and go to heaven and sit in Jesus' lap and listen to the angels sing, Hark, and all that.

That's how I got into the business of dying; by not putting

my foot down. I knew from that first moment when Daddy had me dip my toe down into the cool shade of the water, that this particular teaching exercise would end badly, but because of the dead babies and all, I went along with it.

It goes without saying that Mama was not with me and Daddy at the lake that day and I believe that had she been, this particular fiasco never would have happened in the first place. Mama, by nature is extremely cautious, therefore, I cannot imagine any circumstance in which she would have thought it a good idea to throw me, a child unlearned in the fine art of swimming, into a lake.

But that fateful day, Mama was fulfilling her obligations as day manager of the UPS store, making sure people got their packages weighed, wrapped up tight and paid for so that three days later upon receipt, somebody's day would be made. *Ebay* had just exploded and people were buying used socks and hand-me-down Jadeite ash trays like there was no tomorrow. Consequently, UPS was pressed beyond capacity over into a state of uncomfortable abundance, and Mama, forced to work more hours, was spending considerable less time at home with Daddy and me.

It was a Saturday and Daddy had just fed me eggs for breakfast, two of them sunny side up, even though I would rather have had cereal. *Fruity Pebbles* was and still is my favorite. Here in Heaven, you can have any kind of cereal you want and not just at breakfast, but anytime! A man that looks like the Jesus from my Illustrated Children's Bible serves it up in enormous white mixing bowls. He claims he's not Jesus, just a look-alike and that the real Jesus is busy looking out for the living, who are in constant need of shepherding, and that the

dead are self sufficient and in no need of guidance whatsoever because, well you know, we're dead and just a regular
old waiter will do. Still, I think it's a nice touch that the waiter
looks so holy and all. Kind of like Mary Poppins serving up
your dinner at Disney World; it just adds to the overall mood.

It was early at nine o'clock; ours was the first car in the
parking lot at the marina when we pulled up that morning.
Daddy rented a canoe from a young-adult looking person
running the place whose name tag read, *Hi, I'm Larry. Can I
help?* (If I'd only know how much I was going to need help, I
would have asked Larry very specifically about his services.)

Larry offered us a choice of red canoe or yellow and when
Daddy asked me which one, I shrugged nondescriptly as was
my way and so he picked red even though secretly, I wanted
yellow. After that, it seemed as though there was very little
transitional time between Larry pushing us away from the
dock and Daddy raising up me up high over his shoulders
and yelling, *Bombs away!*, then throwing me overboard.

In retrospect, my first few minutes of struggling above
the water were unremarkable in comparison to what was to
follow, and since I have just poured the milk on my Fruity
Pebbles, I'll focus on the time down below. Funny thing
though, in Heaven cereal never gets soggy. You can literally
pour milk on your cereal in the morning, go off, see-saw all
day, come back, pick up where you left off and the darned
stuff isn't even soft. In fact, its crispier than it was before you
poured the milk on it in the first place! And while we're on
the subject of Heaven, there's no such thing as time here, not
like the time people back on earth count away in seconds and
minutes on watches and classroom clocks. And I guess while

I'm on a roll, it's worth mentioning that in Heaven you never get hungry or cold or tired or anything at all, actually.

In Heaven, you don't have to be afraid of the dark; there is none.

In Heaven, birthday cake doesn't make you fat. There's no such thing as *fat* in Heaven.

In Heaven, watermelon is always in season; there are no seasons.

In Heaven, toothbrushes are unnecessary as cavities do not exist.

In Heaven, Pacman never gets eaten by the ghost. Never. Not even an option.

In Heaven, both The Globe Trotters *and* The Generals win every game.

Also, here in Heaven, there are millions upon millions of cows, just-a-chewing and-a-mooing the day away. They're so soothing to watch, so mesmerizing. I find great pleasure in doing nothing but cow watching for hours-or maybe its minutes or even days. Like I mentioned before, I have no real way of telling. And I promise it's not weird. There's a whole group of us here that gather on a regular bases to observe the antics of the cows. It's like bird watching back on earth, only here it's more reliable. But, back to me dying.

So there I was at *acceptance*, the water swallowing me whole, my soon to be distended body sinking straight down through a cloud of darting Sunfish, though schizophrenic they seemed for no sooner would they retreat after having come back round again, gently pecking my swollen cheeks, in an attempt I suppose, to taste out my particular species.

When I my feet hit bottom, I looked back up toward the

surface for the movement of the paddle; Daddy's sure fire plan to save me if something went wrong. If I ran into trouble, I was to grab the end and give it a little yank. Daddy would feel the motion and pull me up to safety. But where the paddle should have been was only refracted light, the gently curved bottom of the red boat now appearing as if bent in half.

Back on earth, I used to get wrapped up in my TV shows, *The Fresh Prince of Bel Air, Boy meets World,* re-runs of *Saved by the Bell.* In Heaven, we watch People TV. Its on all the time and the best part is that there are never any season ending cliffhangers. Cliffhangers are the worst! And, they happen all the time on earth TV. It's a miserable thing, being left helplessly to wonder the fate of your favorite character after something bad has happened to her, something such as being attacked by Alpine Parrots, or suffering a fall down a slippery mountain side during a monsoon rain, or even getting separated from her Calculus class during a mandatory school trip to Peru.

But in Heaven, there are no cliffhangers because time on earth never stops so the people we watch just keep going on and on and on until their own personal time on earth is done. Now, it's true that you might wonder what's going to happen next to a person in a certain situation, such as when a man is late to a custom tuxedo fitting and he loses his bus pass or when a woman is mugged in a supermarket parking lot by one armed man wearing a, *Frankie says relax* shirt, but seriously, in Heaven, we inhabitants understand that eventually everyone of those folks are going to die and in comparison to the great croak, none of that other piddly stuff matters. Certainty of death replaces cliff-hanger. Easy math.

Also, I watch People TV with a strange detachment I never had back on earth, but I guess thats Heaven for you; you just don't seem to care about anything. For example, recently I was watching a channel starring a girl whose mother was hell bent on washing her mouth out with soap as punishment for a perceived cursing. The girl was falsely accused of course, it was her twin sister who did it and I have no idea why their own mother couldn't tell them apart, but she couldn't and the evil twin just sat there watching, stifling a lop-sided grin as her sister blew bubbles from her mouth between inarticulate fits of screaming, and I was like: *I wonder what kind of soap that is. Irish Spring maybe? Looks kind of like Irish Spring. Or maybe it's that other kind that looks like Irish Spring that I always got confused with Irish Spring. Oh well, I can't remember.*

See what I mean?

But now that I've seen People TV where I've observed about one-million babies being born, weddings performed, elephants falling into holes they have no hope of ever escaping, divorces, rapes, birthday cakes burned only to be iced over then served anyway as well as husbands jumping out from behind corners to scare wives, I can't help but wonder; who was watching me on the day that I died? Could they see it coming? Had they been watching me from the beginning of my life all the way to my end, or had they switched back and forth between me and someone else? Maybe, they came upon me just as Daddy picked me up over his shoulders and like a sack full of unwanted kittens, threw me into the inhospitable waters of Lake Morone.

Or maybe they tuned in as I sank down deep into the mud, felt it like cake batter between my toes; the very moment I knew in my heart that I would never feel anything else ever again. That moment, that instant of certain doom, is when my channel would have gone black, because what happens next is apparently a Moose Lodge secret.

I've asked around, but so far, no one will admit to witnessing the time that led up to my final moments. I'm not morbid or anything. I don't want an accounting of the look on Daddy's face when he first realized I wasn't coming back up (surprise!) or of mine even, or to know how long I *really* held my breath; if I was calm like I remember or if I panicked like I suspect. No, what I really want to know about are the mermaids, transporters marked by naked blue breast, pixie hair cuts, potty mouths and cellular phones.

The state of Oklahoma had enjoyed an unusually wet Spring that year and the normally clear lakes around Tulsa were pregnant and swollen with runoff and silt. Morone was no exception, the bottom of the lake having morphed into a depository solely intended for the collection of mud. It took the three of them to pull me from the muck.

"Tough break, little sister. Life can be so cruel," the first one said, wrestling my foot free from under a rock.

"Yeah, life's a bitch," agreed the second, releasing me from the slender leafed embrace of the Bulrushes.

"Shit. Life is absolute shit," concluded the third, wiping the gunk from her hands onto her tail, then placing a call. "Yea, we've got another one," the mermaid said into the phone. "I don't know, I'll ask her. What's your name sweetheart?" she ordered between smacks of obnoxiously lime green gum.

"Daphne," I managed, my voice sounding strange and other-worldly, like echoes escaping the mouth of a cave.

"Last name, sugar," she said, snapping her fingers impa-
tiently. "We're on a schedule here."

"Johnson. Daphne Johnson."

"Good girl. Age?" More smacking. I reported that I was
eleven, information she repeated into the phone.

"Number Three, Brisbane Court?" she asked. I nodded in
agreement to my home address, information Mama had practically been manic for me to memorize in case of an emergency. "Yep, that's her, we got her. Yea? Well good for her.
We're on our way." She flipped down the phone. "Mother
of pearl, they get younger everyday," she said to no one in
particular.

The three mermaids surrounded me now, an oddly shaped
circle of tails and fins, tattooed arms, tightly cropped blue hair
and what struck me possibly as strangest of all, neon pink
fanny packs, the color of which could only be interpreted as
blinding. Much like the three bears from the Goldilocks tale,
they presented themselves in three distinct shapes and sizes;
first up, the tall, mercilessly skinny one, grooming me like a
mother would.

"Oh, look at you now. Your hair's a mess," she lamented,
smoothing the stray strands away from my face, her long,
slender fingers acting as a comb. "Fastener," she commanded
to the much shorter, plumper one beside her, a mermaid no
taller than me but possessing the equivalent of at least three
times my girth, the strap from her pack visibly struggling to
accommodate the voluptuous demands of her waist.

"Coming right up," she answered, unzipping the pouch to
revel among other things, a stash of elastic hair-bands. The
tall mermaid quickly applied one to my hair, then had me

blow my nose into a tissue she commandeered in the same way.

"You're dead, honey. I know that this comes as such a blow, with you only being eleven and all but frankly, your poor stupid daddy is so dumb I'm surprised he hasn't killed you way before this. Throwing a wee one overboard is no way to teach anyone to swim. It's a good way to help us make our quota, but that's about it. Good there now, that *did* help," she declared, standing back to look at her work.

"That's the truth, Sue," agreed the one with the phone. "He's a fucking idiot, that one. Gum, Lanie."

Again, the short mermaid rummaged through the pack at her waist. After a moment of searching she let out an "ah ha!", then placed a freshly wrapped piece of gum into the outstretched hand of the phone mermaid who in-turn launched the spent gum from her mouth like a rocket, an event proving irresistible to a school of minnows swimming nearby. As the gum sank, the shimmering fish gave chase, nibbling the piece its entire way to the bottom of the lake until it finally disappeared into the mud.

"Shite, I hate this farking flavor," said the cursing, phone-talking, gum-chewing mermaid, smacking on.

At first I was puzzled by such language because, though my world was largely populated by adults, none of them ever spoke to me in what struck me as such a grown up way, but then it occurred to me that while these mermaids were mostly taller than me *and* radiating a certain degree of life experience I would surely never know, they might not be adults at all. Plus, these were not people, these were fish; foul mouthed, fanny pack wearing, gum smacking fish. Who

knew what qualified you for a grown-up in fish land. And
apparently I was dead, so there was that. But I thought I'd
ask anyway, just to make sure. Sue had the kindest face, so I
asked her directly.

"So, I'm dead?"

"Officially."

"And there's no way out of it?"

"No darlin', not when you choose it. And you did, did you
not?"

She had me there, just like daddy's hero Mr. Ben Matlock,
the famous trial lawyer on TV. I *had* chosen it. I was tired-
tired of struggling through the April waters of Lake Morone,
tired of suffocating each time water filled my lungs, tired of
punched out cheeks, flailing limbs, the sound of my own
frenzied screams resonating through-out the chambers of my
head; tired of the desperation ringing round my shoulders
like a one of Mama's plastic ponchos, invariably placed upon
me during days marked with rain.

At the time, it seemed to me that I had no other choice, that
dying was my best and only defense against everything in
my life being forced upon me, and not just the ill-conceived
swimming lessons that were currently doing me in. But from
the thousands of hours of courtroom drama re-runs Daddy
insisted he couldn't watch without me sitting beside him; me
in a near state of comatose boredom, and him, asleep in his
chair by the time the opening credits began to roll.

And headbands, oh my gosh, those horrible, demonic
headbands! Torture devices deceptively disguised by ribbons
and lace, their unguarded ends viscously digging into the
skin behind my ears, rubbing me raw until I bled. "So pretty,"

Mama would chirp like a bird when pressing one upon me. "Mommy's little angel!"

And if that wasn't enough, surely death would defend me from the piano lessons slated to start in the fall, even though twice I had taped pictures of saxophones to the side of the refrigerator in an attempt to sway things my way.

But I didn't feel dead and what's more, I wasn't sure I wanted to be dead all the time, just when it was convenient. Conversely, I also wanted to be alive when it was convenient. Daddy had already promised me donuts on the way home from the lake and *Scooby Doo* would be on by the time we got there. If I was lucky, he would fall asleep in his recliner leaving me unsupervised for most of the day until Mama came home from work demandeding my attention. So, for the first time in my life, I argued.

"I did choose it, but only because I was tired and I think a little angry, (*Anger,* the last of the five stages). But now I've changed my mind, I don't want to be dead. Please. But, thank you anyway."

"Aw, she's very polite, this one. That mother of yours raised you well."

"Thank you," I said quietly. "But I mean it. I really don't want to be dead."

"Hardly anyone does, sweetheart," consoled Lanie, taking a tube of lip-balm from her pack and running it swiftly across her magenta colored lips.

"But I'm only eleven."

She puckered twice, then smacked. "Yea, that's the part that sucks alright. I'll wager you've never even been kissed, not the right way, anyhow."

She was right, I hadn't, but I was too young to know how angry I *should* be.

The cell phone rang.

"Veronica here," the gum-smacker answered. "What have you got? Uh, huh, uh huh. Just keep your hat on, we're a coming; this ones a talker. What's that you say? Those bastards-we'll be right there." She flipped down the phone, let out a swear.

"It's those bastard dolphins," she explained, waving the phone around for dramatic emphasis. "While we've been standing here arguing with this little miss they just took two more from us. We'll never meet our quota standing here like this. Sorry, Daphne Johnson of Number Three, Brisbane Lane, you're dead and that's final. Taint nothing we can do about it."

Sue let out a little sigh. "Tis true, darlin'. We're only the transporters, we don't make the decisions. Pen." To Lanie she held her open hand, the command prompting the mermaid to again explore the contents of her pack. After a series of swear words, she brought out a ball point pen, *Lenny's Dive Shop*, printed across the side. "He's my cousin," she said, by way of an explanation.

"Now sign here, dear," Sue instructed, flipping up the bottom of her tail and pressing it into my hands. What I had conceived from a distance to be tiny scales now revealed themselves up-close as signatures; autographs transcribed in every color ink imaginable, crossed *t*'s and dotted *i*'s, pulsating and glowing, throbbing in swim. Like hypnosis their movement became persuasive and soon I found myself transmuted straight back into my old, complacent self. Without argument I took up the pen, never asking the origins of the names before me, for I knew that like mine, these were names of the dead.

"Thank you," Sue said, taking the pen and handing it back to Lanie. "Lanie, you will witness?"

"Of course, don't I always?" Across my newly registered name Lanie scribbled an ancient looking letter that could have been an *E* professing itself in capital form had it not lacked the required, horizontal line converging through the middle. I watched as our signatures merged into one, the image of a thick, bowline knot becoming the product of their union. "*Now,* its official," she said, replacing the instrument in her pack then zipping it closed.

The Mermaids stood back to look at me. Sue shook her head side to side.

"I'm still not satisfied with her hair, but at least those streaks are fading from her face. All that clawing and crying. And her nose isn't dripping quite as much; so much gooey snot. Here, better take another tissue, dear, just in case. Tuck it into your bosom, there it goes."

"But I haven't even got a bosom," I whimpered, shoving the tissue down the front of my suit. I thought of the bras Mama had gotten forty percent off at *The Little Lady Boutique,* trainers she had put away for later, for when I needed them. Now there would be no later and the *Tiny Cupped Princesses* would forever hang idle and useless in the back of my closet.

Lanie tapped me on the chin. "Chin up dear, you'll want to look your best for when you meet The Hat. That's it, smile."

"The Hat?" I asked, my face working its way through a series of contortions in pursuit of a smile that would not come.

"Maybe we should braid her hair," suggested Sue.

"What about a French knot? I'm terribly good at those, you know," Lanie offered.

"Enough!" yelled Veronica. "I've seen worse, we all have. Now let's get going."

The makeover was over.

"Now listen," Veronica commanded, grabbing my arms. "You were a good kid in life, so you're going to the good place. We're your transporters. We're going to make sure you get through this place-to that place, safe and sound. Now to get there, we've got to swim and God knows you're no good at it, no thanks to that ridiculously stupid father of yours, so I want you to cling unto me and I'll swim you. Sue will be up front, Lanie in back, the two of us in the middle. But you, little miss, you've got to promise to keep your eyes closed the entire way through, because *The Blue* ain't no place for a child and I'll have none of your peekin'. Even if you feel something come and grab you, or you hear a scream that sends your scales to crawlin', you're not to open your eyes. You got me, little sister?" she asked, leaning in close and holding a fist to my face. I moved back as if already struck, shaking my head vigorously to indicate that I did.

"Good," she barked. " Ladies, formations!" Sue and Lanie fell into line.

"Everyone in positions?"

"Ready!" Came voices unified.

Then came the announcement:

"Here this, all you Slimies! Tis Veronica who's speaking to you. I'm now wrapping Daphne Johnson, age eleven of Number Three, Brisbane Court. She is spoken for in the afterlife and we aim to transport her. If you interfere, you will die. Any questions?"

The lake became silent and frozen; the gentle, clipping waves of the water quieted, the nibbling of the Sunfish ceased. Satisfied, the mermaid nodded, then began the miraculous act of wrapping me.

"Arms!" she commanded and so they did grow; six new appendages bursting through the dappled material of her ribcage, a sound like thawing ice retreating a roof-top serenading this most unusual birth.

"Come to me, darlin'," she said, offering me the whole flock of hands. "Good girl," she called me, as I nestled my head between her breast.

"Braid!" she commanded and in an instant the multitude obeyed, swaddling the two of us together in an impossibly intricate pattern, the conjoining intimate and cocoon-like in affect.

Tails!, came next, Veronica's own dividing into three separate entities; inexplicable beasts spinning around us like ribbon to a spool. In that moment I became like one of Mama's packages, carefully and meticulously wrapped, ready for delivery.

And last came the wings. Time and again I've been asked to more fully recount them but I can't, because so far as I know, there are no words to explain such a miracle. So don't ask me to elaborate when I tell you that they were made of waterfalls and sparkled like sunlight passing through rainbows; that's the best I can do. I'm sure my eyes became like gaping holes as I first gazed upon their impossible beauty.

"Are you angels?" I asked, thinking I finally knew the

answer to a question.

Veronica shook her head sideways, sympathy for my stupidity reading like a script across her face. "You poor, daft child. We're mermaids, nothing more, nothing less. Now close your eyes and don't open them till we have delivered you safe into the arms of The Hat."

Have you ever been aware of your lashes gently grazing your face on any one of the millions of occasions you've closed your eyes? I swear to you that those seemingly insignificant little hairs fell upon me with a weight so oppressive that shudders like fever shakes reverberated throughout my entire body causing me to cry out as if wounded.

"There child, I give you my word. Faith," Veronica told me, her voice slipping into a place of comfort, "is what will get us there." I felt her lips on my cheek; the undeniable mark of a kiss. Like Menthol on sunburn it burned, terrible and soothing, all at the same time.

I am proud to report to you that I kept my eyes closed the entire way through The Blue, even when the grabbers grabbed and the screamers screamed. Even, perhaps most impressively, when from in front of us Sue called out in warning.

"God almighty! Would you look at the size of that Kraken! Lanie, ax!" And felt the handle brush right past me on its way forward into battle.

I kept my eyes closed even when Sue announced that we were out of harms way and by the sound and the movement, could tell that we were on an elevator going up, Bob Dylan coming through on the speakers, his version of "Knockin' on Heavens Door," playing softly in the background as the mermaids checked each other for wounds.

"I thought it would be something more reverent," I said, referring to the song.

"Nah," Lanie answered. "Dylan's a treasure. That other stuff just gets on your nerves after awhile. Now hold still Sue, you've got a claw sticking out your back."

"Son of a-Ahh, shite!" Sue groaned. "Why do they never hurt till you pull em out?" It was a question no one bothered to answer.

Still, I kept my promise and didn't open my eyes when the electronic bell rang announcing our destination, or even when the door to the elevator slid open and a wave of water rushed past us spilling out like a down pour from a gutter. I didn't open my eyes until Veronica said I that could. Tenderly, she unwrapped me, bonus arms retracting, segregated tails like the ending lanes of a highway, merging back seamlessly into one.

Like my mother did on the first day of kindergarten, gently, she pushed me forward. "Daphne Johnson of Number Three, Brisbane Lane, meet, The Hat."

"Well done as always!" he said, rushing forward to greet me, at the same time clapping in a way that could only be described as extremely enthusiastic. "And punctual too! Let's have a look at her." Placing his hands atop my shoulders he spun me a full rotation; satisfied, he resumed the mad-cap applause.

"Excellent, all there, ladies! I'll gladly sign."

Lanie presented the pen and Sue her tail and The Hat, taking both in his hands, quickly scribbled out an exact representation of the headpiece worn atop his head.

Then came a bang!

And a pop!

A cloud of smoke rose up from the spot then quickly fizzled out into nothing, as if no smoke had ever been there at all.

Lanie returned the pen to her pack, Sue her tail to the ground and to all, The Hat gave a courteous salute.

The Hat.

He was a man and a woman and a child and a dog and a city and a freshly buttered ear of sweet, summer corn. He was the first bird of springtime, a trick-or-treat bag filled beyond capacity with nothing but chocolates. He was a festively wrapped gift sitting under a sparkling Christmas tree.

The Hat was a movie screen and a ballet, the see-saw in the park and a warm blanket on a cold winters night. He was a harvest moon, a mewing calico kitten, an every-color striped beach umbrella fully opened and casting shadows on the ground. He was golden, glittering sand, damp and pressed into a bucket just right, just perfectly right; he was the castle poured out, whose borders the tide would never reach.

The Hat was a saxophone realized.

The Hat was Saturday morning cartoons.

From different angles he was anything, *everything*, and as he spun making circles and slid into slides, motions I now know as almost constant to Heaven's longest serving concierge, I saw it all. But mostly, from the front, when he was still for those rare, brief fleeting moments, he was just a person, dead, like me.

But in all those things, all those variations, the one constant was his hat. Born of resplendent silk, the enormous top hat spun when he clapped, though never disappeared when he did-a half spin to the left for one short, fast staccato-like bringing together of his hands, a turn and a half to the right for two. For those times when chains of applause rolled from his hands, the hat would spin endlessly like a never ceasing top.

"Welcome to Heaven my dear one, and didn't Sue do a fine job with your hair. I for one, have always thought that a pony-tail makes its wearer look so perky!" He offered me his hand and as I gave him my own he was *Scooby Doo* and donuts mounded with sprinkles and a long afternoon of freedom narrated by the happy sounds of a snoring father in a worn out chair.

He bowed to my transporters. "Thank you, Maighdean na Tuinne. I will see you soon."

The mermaids nodded, then retreated back into the elevator. Veronica's phone rang and she answered.

"Veronica here, who died now?" There was a slight pause while she listened. "Really? And in the bath? Not much of a surprise I don't suppose, not after what he did to his poor child. And you say there's no head left at all? That'll cost you extra, especially where that one's going."

Lanie pushed the *down* button. Sue gave me a little wave. The doors shut. The mermaids were gone.

Everyone in Heaven has their own transportation story. My friend Holly, who died in a plane crash, swears she was brought here by eagles, birds she can only describe as great rumbling clouds of black thunder.

Lewis, who died in a high rise apartment fire, claims he was transported by an enormous bear who spoke hypnotically into the flames; *you do not know me, you do not know me.*

Jerry was a bus driver who fell asleep at the wheel driving

a group of seniors to an Indian Casino. His transporter drove a chariot made from the sun whose license plate read, *Sol Invictus*, while his bronzed arm unapologetically displayed the tattoo, *Daddy's boy*. When Jerry first laid eyes upon The Hat, he saw him first as a cool glass of water and only then as a man.

No two people in Heaven seemed to have had the same transporters. Even those who died together were transported separately; those who perished in the same way were delivered by different haulers.

Every time a drowner arrives I ask them about my mermaids, but so far, there is still no sign of those foul mouthed fish; the motherly Sue, the voluptuous Lanie, my protector, Veronica. Sometimes I wonder if I ever knew them at all, or if they were just things, things I thought I saw in the water.

And People TV is no help either. So far, I've yet to hear of a transporter sighting there at all. The minute a situation goes south for some poor sap their channel goes dark, then switches over to a birthday party, and without fail, it's always a *baby's first*. I guess whoever is in charge of programming figures we never get tired of seeing an overstimulated bald-headed baby stick a fist full of blue frosting into his mouth for the first time. They're wrong of course, we *do* get tired of it, but the thing about Heaven is that you have no desire to complain, so sometimes we get taken advantage of. But there again, we don't mind. On earth people would call it a viscous cycle, but here in Heaven, we just call it "that baby thing again."

But even with so many different tales of shipment, all of our stories have two things in common; no one peeked during their time in *The Blue*, no one, and everyone's journey ended with an upward bound elevator ride, sounding bells and Bob Dylan announcing the end of a pilgrimage, and the start of something new.

So, I don't know how you'll get here, but I know that when the time is right, you will. I've been watching your channel and you've got a lot going for you! You're kind, honest, pious in a humble way; you're doing just fine. And may I commend your doctors because they never gave up on you and it's a good thing too or we never would have gotten to have this pep talk.

I've enjoyed our visit but it's time for you to wake up now, because though it may seem like it, your number isn't up yet. You're just having a little hiccup in what is otherwise a lovely little life. No, ma'am, no five stages of loss for you yet! Don't forget, on your way out, please fill out a, *How did I do?* card, and I hope you'll give me high marks. It's my first day working as a counselor here in **The Office of Near Death Experiences**, and truthfully, I'm a little nervous; I've never had a job before. I think I might have talked too much about myself. Sorry, I do that sometimes. And I apologize as well for eating my cereal while chatting, but you know, old habits and all that.

But one last thing before you go, if you see my mother, please tell her that I said "Hi," and that I'm doing just fine, really, I am, so not to worry.

And for Pete's sake, whatever you do, don't throw your kid into the lake.

ACKNOWLEDGEMENTS

Writing is a solitary venture. Please understand that for me at least, it isn't lonely, the constant cast of characters in my head seeing to that. So, while the act of writing is done alone, the acts of reading, discussing and editing are not and to that end I am extremely grateful to the following people: To my readers, thank you, Kelly Ann-Go OU!-Duke, Jessica and Mary Kate Bartnik, sisters whose literary prowess is the modern day equivalent to that of the Bronte's, and Doctor Antoinette Johnson, who can mark up a manuscript faster than most people can read one thanks to her mad professor skills. To all, your finely tuned reading skills and enthusiasm were invaluable.

Thank you Jeremy Foster-Fell for taking a chance on me, not once, but twice in this lifetime and Jera Foster-Fell for using your immense talents so generously in order to make this project come together so beautifully. I am eternally grateful to you both.

Many heartfelt thanks to my mother, Shirley Lamb Frazier, for her keen insights and inspiring support, to my sister, Melanie Frazier Rock who is the toughest woman I know and who, on more than one occasion has reminded me to be so, and to my own sons, Noah and Sam, young men whom I truly believe think it is nothing short of normal for their mother to sit around for hours a day making up stories and writing them down. Bless you both. (To be fair, it *is* normal for me). And to Chris, my first reader, editor and partner in all things, whose love of simple, clean vernacular constantly keeps me challenged, I thank you. And finally to my creator, the one who drew this path for me and waited patiently for me to follow.

CPSIA information can be obtained at www.ICGtesting.com
Printed in the USA
BVOW02s0703220715

409850BV00014B/117/P